HEATER

MW00583573

# Heather

## CHRIS KENISTON

Indie House Publishing

Indie House Publishing

# BOOKS BY CHRIS KENISTON

*Hart Land*
Heather
Lily
Violet
Iris

*Farraday Country*
Adam
Brooks
Connor
Declan
Ethan
Finn
Grace
Hannah
Ian
Jamison
Keeping Eileen

*Aloha Series Closed Door Edition*
Aloha Texas
Almost Paradise
Mai Tai Marriage
Dive Into You
Look of Love
Love by Design
Love Walks In
Flirting with Paradise

# ACKNOWLEDGEMENTS

I am so happy to finally bring you the first of a new series that has been tickling the back of my mind ever since an afternoon on a Maui balcony with my cohort in brainstorming, Cheryl Lucas. The flowers, amongst other things, are all her idea!

The medical parts of this story were a challenge and a half. For the accuracy of the complex surgery and hospital life, I thank Kathy Ivan and Liz Lipperman, both wonderful authors and friends. For the mistakes, well, those are all mine!

With the reality of life, and health, and family being ever intrusive, I have Barb Han to thank for our weekly writing sessions and keeping my muse moving. You rock!

A special thanks to my Aunt Mary, for being an outstanding baker and willing to share her recipes with the world!

To all my fans who have patiently waited for Heather, thank you. Y'all are truly an author's dream!

*"It will never work."*
*"Of course, it will."*
*"As much as I'd like to think you're right, I don't know."*
*"Well, I do. Sit back and see for yourself."*

# CHAPTER ONE

For the second time in twenty-four hours, baby Kyle had coded. His heart simply couldn't take the stress of pumping blood into his little body any longer.

On the heels of two early morning surgeries, and bolstered only by a tall cup of coffee and a twenty-minute power nap, Dr. Heather Preston finished her meticulous scrub routine. Her mind thinking through every carefully planned step of the longshot surgery.

Born with a rare congenital valve malformation, the baby was scheduled for surgery next week when the chief of cardio-thoracic surgery returned from his trip to Geneva. But this last failure had forced Heather's hand; they couldn't wait for Dr. Michaelson. She would have to step in as lead surgeon. Pulling this off would take a miracle, and even with the best surgical team any doctor could ask for—she was still banking on a whopper.

It was time. Through the OR doors, baby Kyle fought for his life as heparin dripped to stop his blood from clotting in the heart-lung machine. Hip checking the door, Heather entered the room, hands in the air, and the circulating nurse did her gown and gloves then tied the mask.

"Time to get this show on the road." Through the mask her voice held a note of extra sunshine. Only positive thoughts.

The perfusion team was ready and waiting, having already set up the complex array of equipment to keep Kyle's body alive when his heart was stopped.

*When his heart was stopped.* The magnitude of those five simple words kept Heather forever thankful for the daily miracles that came to pass when a repaired heart beat again. They would do this.

"Jim has a surprise for you." Betty, her best scrub nurse smiled.

Jim Taylor, never using his full first name James in order to avoid jokes about the famous singer, was a phenomenal anesthesiologist. She was eternally grateful he would be sitting at the helm for this.

"Thought I'd change things up a bit today." Jim said. "Mozart may be good for the brain, but I woke up humming 'Don't Stop Believing'."

"Journey?" That was a surprise indeed.

"My wife gave me a CD."

For as long as she'd worked at this man's side he'd chosen the tranquil, calming—and occasionally snoozeable—sounds of classical music. Journey would be...different.

The familiar sounds of a well-choreographed team echoed from the first cut to the peeling back of the pericardial membrane. Betty, who'd worked so well with Heather they might as well have been one body, sucked in an audible breath and muttered aloud what every person watching thought—*damn it*. A heart they'd expected to be the size of the patient's fist was so enlarged it would have been more suitable pumping life into an elementary-aged child, and yet, it was too scarred to pump for tiny Kyle. An already complex procedure just got a whole helluva lot harder.

The signal to go on bypass given, technology took over and an empty little heart waited for reconstruction. For every cut of the malformation, the following stitch had to be precise, accurate, and better than watertight.

Within hours of stopping the heart, they were ready for blood to flow again. Removing the clamp that had stemmed the flow, the pale pink heart quickly turned dark. *Crap.*

What had they missed? She'd checked for bleeding.

"He's in V-tach," Jim called out. The EKG monitor showed the erratic activity.

Breathing deeply to still her own rapid heartbeat, the order had to be given. "Ten joules." The sound of an electric shock directly through the muscle to restore normal rhythm snapped in the air. Her heart hurting, knowing odds were not in Kyle's favor, Heather and the entire team stared, breath held. Nothing. *Damn it.* "Shock it again!" *Come on, Kyle.*

Still no reaction. Too much scar tissue for the tiny heart to handle. And now, a mitral valve leak was visible. *Hell on a broomstick.* Where had that come from? They couldn't keep him on bypass forever and with no response the odds of any recovery were tanking fast. There wasn't a choice. She'd have to cut some more. It was a risk, but a high risk was better than no chance at all.

Cutting away as much additional scar tissue as she dared, and having stitched the central point in a best effort to stem the mitral leak, Heather lifted her hands and drew from that last drop of emotional strength she stored up for days like today. Time to defibrillate and pray for a normal rhythm. "We're done. Twenty joules."

"Clear." All eyes on the tiny heart. A second felt like an hour, and then she saw it—a flicker on the overhead screen. A long held breath, and like flipping a switch, Kyle's heart muscle contracted in response. "Yes!"

Fatigue slipped away and adrenaline took its place. Almost four hours on bypass and not a moment to spare, she gave the order. "Come off slowly." Stripping her gloves and walking away, Heather's own heart did a joyful dance. She'd have stood on her aching feet with nothing but bad coffee and a prayer from now till the next millennium if it would have helped.

Now, God willing, and as her Grams would add *"if the Creek don't rise,"* one more child would make it home and grow up with his family. Life didn't get any better than this.

• • • •

Some days didn't want to cut a man a break. The brick building that housed the family hardware store was indestructible—not so much the ancient plumbing. Jake Harper had spent the better part of the morning curled into the cabinet under the bathroom sink. How he'd never noticed that in all the generations before him no one had ever installed a shut off valve was beyond him.

Now, he stood balancing the new window air conditioning unit in his office in an effort to secure it before he and everything in the hundred and twenty square foot room melted under today's unseasonal spike in temperature.

"Whoa." Jake's right-hand man stepped into the blistering office. "This place is hotter than the sandbox in July."

"Tell me something I don't know."

"Got the floor in the bathroom mopped up and the shipment of blades and cutters you've been waiting for finally arrived."

"About time." Jake turned the knob to full blast and took a step back, basking in the quiet rumble and cool air blowing from the small contraption. "Much better."

"Shh," Tom chuckled. "Don't say anything or something else might break."

Earlier today, Jake had barely sat down to work on incoming inventory when the a/c unit in his office gave a sizzle and spark performance worthy of ringing in the New Year. Leaping to his feet, he'd barely unplugged the thing before it caught fire when Tom burst into the room announcing the cascading pipes. The only thing working in his favor was having the bathroom tucked far enough into a warehouse corner that the small flood didn't have time to do any collateral damage to stored inventory.

The ding of the front door opening sounded and Jake spun about. "You take a well-deserved break; I'll take care of the customer."

Lawford was a small community on one of New England's best hidden lakes. There were plenty of new faces when the tourists swept in during the summer season to vacation but otherwise, Jake knew just about every local resident. Some since he was a kid working the register at his dad's side. Sadie Norton was no exception. Though until his passing about a year or so ago, it was Mr. Norton who always popped into the hardware store.

"How can I help you, Mrs. Norton?"

The petite woman glanced up from the wall of hammers and offered him a shaky smile meant to show confidence. "I'm going to fix my sink."

Jake did his best to smother an amused smile. There wouldn't be much she could do to her sink with a hammer. "What seems to be the problem?"

"I'm tired of emptying the bucket under the U-tube."

It actually took Jake a second to realize she meant the P-trap. "I see."

Her gaze scanned the varying types of hammers and skimmed over to nearby saws. "I'm thinking I need one of those plumber thingies."

Okay, he might have figured out P-trap, but it was more his own knowledge of plumbing than her explanation that had him guessing. "You want a pipe wrench."

Eyes wide with confusion suddenly twinkled with satisfaction, and she bobbed her head. "Yes. That's what I need."

"Have you tried calling Mike's Plumbing? I'm sure one of his guys could pop by in a minute and fix it for you."

The light in her eyes dimmed. "He's too busy for something so simple. My Bill would fix those things in a heartbeat. I'm sure I'll figure it out."

Or break something, including an arm. "You know, I'm leaving here in a few minutes, going to stop by the grocery and pick up a frozen dinner. I could go by your place on the way and fix that up in a jiffy."

"Frozen dinner. Nonsense." Her face lit up with something akin to delight. "You come straight over, and while you fix the sink, I'll whip you up a good hot meal."

"If it's not too much trouble, that would be a nice change."

Straightening her shoulders, her grip tightened on her purse and her smile spread across her face. "Yes. I'm sure it will. I'd better hurry."

Jake was still watching the older woman scurry away when he almost heard Tom shaking his head.

"You do remember we have a freezer full of home cooked meals in the back."

Jake turned and smiled at his friend since kindergarten. How could he forget? There wasn't enough room in his own freezer at home for all the homemade foods he'd collected as payment over the last few months from the growing list of seniors struggling with home repairs. "What's one more sink to fix today? You don't mind closing up for me, do you?"

"Nope." Tom shook his head. Like anyone else who'd been deployed overseas by the Marine Corps, Tom understood the concept of a little sacrifice to help others in need. "Go fix her sink. You may want to look around for a few other things in disrepair while you're there. Her husband always seemed to be in here holding that old house of theirs together with spit, a little ingenuity, and a prayer. It may be falling down around her by now."

"That's exactly what I had in mind." He'd have to add Ms. Norton to his list. Like he told Tom, what was a little more time tucked under a sink? After a day like today there was one thing he was sure of—sleep tonight would come nice and easy.

• • • •

Right about now Heather needed a good hard slap in the face—or a cold shower—or maybe both. The probability of getting enough sleep to wake up actually feeling human again made the odds *slim to none* sound favorable.

During her internship she'd come to terms with absurdly long hours. Then, as a resident, functioning on sheer adrenaline and coffee had become a way of life. She'd come to accept long hours on her feet and cat naps on sofas as her forever normal—even more so since working with Doctor Michaelson.

Satisfied baby Kyle was stable, for now, she adjusted the pager on her hip and strolled into the break room. Waving to one of the cardiac fellows, she tipped her head in the direction of the pot. "Fresh?"

The woman offered a friendly smile. "No, but it's strong."

"Works for me." She poured herself a cup.

"Done for the day?"

Breathing in the familiar aroma of bad coffee, Heather nodded. After Kyle they'd had to wheel the 8:30am surgery back in for a second time. She was overdone.

"Then why aren't you on your way to the parking lot?"

"I could ask you the same thing." Lifting a shoulder in a half-hearted shrug, Heather was too tired to make the effort at hefting both shoulders and blew out a sigh. "You know how it is. I'm going to put my feet up and rest my eyelids in the on-call room, just in case we need to go back in on Kyle." Yeah, she was still just a tad worried. She'd feel much better when the sweet baby was at least forty-eight hours post op. "You, however, should go home and get some sleep. Tomorrow is an early start."

The other woman threw back the last drop of coffee and staring down at the empty cup, shook her head. "Some days the coffee just isn't strong enough to keep up."

Amused by the departing words but too tired to laugh, Heather collapsed onto the well-worn sofa. She wouldn't be the first or last doctor to forego a good night's sleep in her own bed in case a patient needed her—fast. Fishing in her pocket, she pulled out her phone and debated if there was any point to going home to her own bed only to have to turn around and come back for the morning's surgery schedule.

Sliding her thumb over the glass screen, she hissed out a sigh. Not one, not two, but ten missed calls. Almost all from her family.

The first two were from the lake house. That would be her Grandmother. The woman had a cell phone but rarely remembered to charge or carry it. A few from her sister, Violet and one from her sister Rose. A smattering from her cousins Iris and Lily. But the final missed call from the General himself, her grandfather, was the one that had her stomach pitch left then right before springing into a full-blown somersault.

"Blast." If her phone was correct, and of course there was no reason to believe it wasn't, time had gotten away from her—again. Lately the General had been calling often to remind her about Sunday dinner at the lake house, and every time she'd promise to do her best to make it. Growing up, having the family all home when the General was in house was the biggest deal. Attendance was not requested, it was expected. Her aunt Marissa would pack up Iris and Zinnia, swing by Boston to pick up Heather's mom with Rose, Violet and of course Heather in tow. The two sisters would grumble all the way to the lake and then spend the weekend with their sister Virginia and her four daughters, laughing and promising to stay longer next time. By the time the General retired, Sunday suppers were pretty much compulsory, but as his granddaughters had all grown up, the frequent dinners had become merely open door policy. Come if you can. The exception: the last Sunday of the month. Six days from now.

Blowing out a long slow sigh, she closed her eyes, summoning the stamina to return the call. No nap. Her only reprieve, stalling long enough to call the land line first knowing her grandmother would be the one to answer. Since the General worshipped the ground his wife of decades walked on, reaching out to Grams before calling his cell would be the only acceptable delay that wouldn't bring censure down with a boom.

The phone rang twice before the line clicked to life.

"Hello?"

"Hi Grams, how are you?"

"Hello, dear." Two simple words and the warmth of the familiar voice soothed her tired soul. "We're hoping to see you this weekend."

"I know, but there's a fellow shadowing our group this month from France and Dr. Michaelson is stacking back to back surgeries for all of us like sardines in a can. "

"You do sound tired. Are you getting enough sleep? Eating right?"

The barrage of concern made Heather smile. She glanced over at the coffee pot and estimated the warm sludge she'd inhaled most likely did not constitute eating right. "I could use a nap."

"Lily's been testing new recipes for chocolate cake."

*Ooh, hitting below the belt.* Her cousin Lily had managed to produce the most delectable confections since her first Easy Bake Oven. Though her cousin's kolackys were hard to resist, chocolate cake was Heather's weak spot and Grams knew it. She couldn't blame her grandmother for going straight for the chocolate jugular. If she had a normal nine to five job, she'd be on her way to the lake right now, but life, her life, especially, was beyond busy. There simply weren't enough hours in the day. Certainly not in days like this one. Escaping to the lake wasn't an option. Not even for Lily's latest chocolate cake creations.

In the distance a husky, male voice boomed, "Fiona?"

"I'm on the phone, dear."

"With who?"

"It's Heather, dear."

Before anyone could say another word, the General had picked up an extension and muttered her name through a momentary coughing fit.

The unexpected sound took Heather by surprise. "Are you feeling okay, General?"

"Never better," he rumbled. "We've missed you at dinner. It's been a while."

"I'm sorry. You know how things go."

"I don't." The older man tried to muffle another cough. "But I might if we ever saw you." Her grandfather's brusque tone might have concerned her more if she wasn't so fixated on why the man who never seemed to have caught even the common cold in his entire life was now trying not to hack up a lung.

"Grams, do you mind if I talk to the General for a bit?"

"Not at all. I love you, sweetie." The extension disconnected and her grandfather coughed harder, and this time louder.

"I don't like the sound of that." Anyone else and she wouldn't have given a cough a second thought.

"It's nothing. Frog in my throat. I want to make sure you'll be here for dinner on Sunday."

She knew better than to let her grandfather deflect the conversation. "Have you been to see Dr. Wilkins?"

"That old coot? He doesn't know what ends up."

"So you've seen him?"

"I didn't say that."

"But you have. What did he say that you didn't like?" She asked more firmly this time.

"Are you coming to dinner or aren't you?"

"You forgot your pills, dear," her grandmother's voice sounded in the distance.

Pills? She really didn't like the sound of this. The man didn't even believe in vitamins. Holding her breath, she quickly considered her options. Grilling the former military man on the phone would get her nowhere fast. With a little—okay a lot—of careful tap dancing, she could rearrange things at the hospital well enough to get away a few days and see what was going on for herself. Even if it was just a cold, with a man as stubborn as General Harold Hart USMC RET, pneumonia could easily become a concern if he didn't take care of himself.

"Well, young lady?" he groused.

Only her grandfather could make one of the city's most revered surgeons feel like a twelve year old caught stealing her first kiss on the family back porch. "I'll be home Saturday." *Sooner if she could make it happen.*

Warmth seeped into her grandfather's tone. "That's my girl."

Instantly, the cool deep voice of praise settled her nerves. Already feeling better about rearranging her schedule, and looking forward to a lot of chocolate cake, she smiled. Maybe soon she'd finally get a decent night's sleep.

# CHAPTER TWO

"**S**o it's true?"

Only a few days after her grandfather's call, Heather turned off the highway onto Lawford's main drag and rolled her eyes at her sister on the other end of the line. "Not you too?"

"Me too what?" Violet asked.

"It's a three hour drive from the city, and so far I've heard from half the family tree. If the ride were any longer I'd probably hear from the other half as well. I'm spending a couple of days at the lake, not boarding a rocket to Mars."

"Almost the same thing," her sister teased. "I mean, you have to admit, it's been months since the last time you showed up for dinner and even then, Grams hadn't had time to serve dessert before you turned around and drove back to work."

"It was an emergency and time was—"

"Of the essence. Yeah," Violet chuckled, "we know, and we all love you for it, but the last few years your life is always a matter of life and death. You can't blame us for being a bit surprised by the sudden shift in free time."

Thankfully, baby Kyle was so improved she felt more steady about leaving Boston. "It's not like *you're* up here every week."

"No, but I do usually make it for the last Sunday dinner of the month. There's no such thing as a life and death yoga emergency that would pass muster with the General."

Heather laughed into the phone. The General—after all no one would dare call him Grandfather, never mind Gramps—had trained his grandchildren well. Family time was sacred. But that wasn't all her grandfather's doing. Her six cousins were as much sisters to her as Violet and Rose. Getting together with them wasn't a hardship, and maybe the cousins who actually lived year-round at the lake, would have some answers for her about her grandfather's health. "I'd love to keep talking but I'm almost there."

"Okay, see you on Sunday."

"On Sunday." Wasn't that a riot? The two of them lived in the same city and they had to drive to the lake to see each other.

Turning up the road, seeing the white, sprawling main house with its Victorian porch and rows of hedges instantly warmed her heart. The croquet set always set up in the front lawn only added to the charm. She allowed herself to breathe in the still, country air and savored just how different it was from the bustling fumes of city life. She seriously needed to make the time to come home more often. And that was something else she, her sisters, and their cousins had in common. Raised in different cities, even though they'd only spent summers together full time at the lake, each of them considered the old place home.

Scanning the massive front porch for any signs of her grandparents, the mere sight of the dark green rockers swaying with the afternoon breeze gave her heart a kick. She really did love this place. Grabbing her bag from the back seat, she hauled it up the wide steps. Not bothering to knock, she stepped inside just in time to catch sight of her grandfather standing in the middle of the living room balancing a massive box in his arms.

Pivoting for a better view of the front door, he teetered to one side, did a semi pirouette and for a split second she thought he was going to lose the battle with his balance and fall over.

Before she had time to run her mind down the list of possibilities for what combined with old age had coughing and dizziness as symptoms, she dropped her bag with a thud, bolted across the entry hall, and grabbed his arm, grappling for control of the heavy stash. Lady and Sarge, her grandfather's two golden retrievers, stood growling like sentinels on either side of her.

"What do you think *you're* doing?" her grandfather barked in his military officer voice.

"I could ask you the same question." She tugged once more at the box, carefully studying his face for any additional sign of distress.

"I'm retired. Not decrepit." He won the battle of the box and pulled away from her.

The two dogs shifted closer. Their tails wagging, she mindlessly patted one on the head, ignoring the rough tongue washing on her hand and studied the stubborn old man before her. Pleased to see him standing steady with clear speech and focused gaze, the physician in her still wanted to hammer a hundred questions at him. The two wagging tails swishing at her grandfather's feet told her the wobbly moment wasn't critical, but she still wished she could check his blood pressure and heart rate. "Of course you're not decrepit, but you have staff to help with heavy lifting." She glanced around. "Where is George anyhow?"

"His niece is getting married this weekend so he's taking a long early vacation." The General set the box down on top of a stack of similar sized boxes.

"What is all this?"

"Your grandmother has decided tatting isn't for her. She's donating her supplies to the nursing home across the lake."

Who knew tatting supplies could be so heavy. "Are there any more?"

"This was the last of them." A cough punctuated the end of his sentence.

"How long have you had the cough?"

"I don't have a cough. Just a frog in my throat." Another cough escaped despite her grandfather's efforts to stifle it.

"Yes, I can see that." Heather blew out an exasperated breath. She could also see the man had lost some weight. Another symptom to add to her list.

One white bushy brow shot up higher than the other, the General's piercing gaze a wordless censure of her sarcasm. Even at his age and a few pounds lighter, standing just over six feet tall, with a broad back and strong shoulders, no man, or granddaughter, would dare to challenge him. A long silent moment passed before the superior officer took a backseat to loving grandfather once again. "Your grandmother is on the back porch with Hyacinth. You go on and say hello and I'll take your bag up to your room."

"That's all right, I can—"

Another glare flew in her direction and Heather realized as grown up as she was, pulling medical rank over this man was going to be harder than she thought. "Yes, sir."

Part of her wanted to tackle the older man and insist he sit through an exam. At least let her take his blood pressure and listen to his lungs. The other part of her knew tackling a grizzly might be more productive and moving on to plan B would make more sense, so she did the only thing a smart, competent, disciplined woman could do—make her way through the kitchen in search of backup.

"I don't believe my eyes," Lucy, the housekeeper and cook who had been with the family since before Heather was born, exclaimed. "Ms. Fiona said you'd be coming, but I didn't believe it."

Before Heather could respond, she found herself in a bone crushing hug. Memories of being a scared little girl on a stormy night and Lucy holding her close, telling funny stories, played like an old movie in her mind. Just like the comforting gesture had done all those years ago, her tensions and worries dimmed.

"You'd better go see your grandmother."

One more quick squeeze and Heather moved outside to find her cousin Hyacinth—Cindy to anyone younger than her parents—seated, elbows on the card table, hands up like a referee at a football game, and their Grams wrapping yarn around them.

Heather would be eternally grateful to her Aunt Virginia for declaring her daughter, born only a few months after Heather, would be named Hyacinth. Through the years her sisters Violet and Rose had fielded enough jokes and teasing over having the same names as Mrs. Bucket of British comedy fame's sisters. Had Heather been named Hyacinth, the jokes would have never ended.

"Well, Callie said you'd be coming, but I don't think I believed her." The bright grin covering Cindy's face gave away the love behind the tease.

"Not you too?" Not sure how Callie—Calytrix by birth—knew of her visit, Heather gave an exaggerated roll of her eyes as she strolled past her cousin, turned and stuck her tongue out like she would have when she was ten years old, then leaned over to give her grandmother a kiss on the cheek and a fast hug.

"It's nice to have you home." Grams set the yarn on the table and pushed to her feet. With her sleek silver hair, porcelain doll complexion, and infectious smile, Fiona Hart was the only woman Heather knew who could get away with wearing a paisley caftan.

"Does your grandfather know you're here?"

Heather nodded. "Met him in the entry, moving boxes."

"Yes. Such a dear. I'll see about getting us a couple of glasses of lemonade. Pull up a chair." Grams turned to face Cindy. "You stay put. I'll be right back."

Cindy nodded and Heather waited for her grandmother's back to disappear into the house before addressing her cousin. "How did Grams get you away from the animal clinic in the middle of the day and rope you into this?"

"I've been asking myself the same thing. There's a feral cat living under the porch who has had what we think is her second litter. Lucy has been working on that feline for months and with the kittens ready to be weaned, Grams finally managed to coax mama kitty into a kennel. I'm going to take her and the kittens back to the clinic. I'll spay her and find good homes for them all."

"So, you're here to pick up the cats?" Heather asked.

Still holding her hands upright in the touchdown position, Cindy nodded.

"And the yarn thing is just—"

"Grams being Grams," Cindy finished the sentence, the two women chuckling at the mutual understanding. "I am, however, getting a free midweek dinner out of the deal."

"There you go." Heather leaned back in the chair.

Arms still spread wide holding the yarn taut, Cindy leaned forward, glanced quickly over each shoulder and skewered Heather with a pointed glare. "I love you, cuz, but there's no way you'd show up at the lake on short notice just to say hi. What the hell is wrong?"

• • • •

"Do you mean to tell me you've been hanging on to both aces this whole time?" the General barked at Jake from across the table.

Any other man would have cowered under the General's brusque demeanor, but having grown up spending most of his summers, along with half the kids in town, playing and hanging out at Hart House Jake understood that was just his way.

"You'll want to eat this, dear." Smiling, Mrs. Hart pushed his plate of chocolate cake closer to him. "I've often thought if we could just get world leaders to sit down over cake they wouldn't be so grumpy."

Jake chuckled softly, picking up his fork before taking a huge bite of the cake. After all, last slice or not, he wasn't one to look Lily's fudge cake in the mouth.

"Are we going to talk cake or play Whist?" Lily, the baker in the family, raised her eyebrows from her grandparents to Jake.

He had no idea how often Lily played with her grandparents and their friends, but the girl was a card shark if ever there was one. Which, possibly, was why she was looking at Jake like he'd just lost his mind.

"Play cards." The General tapped his finger on the table at Jake. "And pay attention."

Lily repressed a snort of laughter.

From the table across the porch, Ralph, their friend and neighbor, leaned away from his own card game. "Now, Harold. This is Jake's first time coming around to play in years, don't go chasing him away. We could use some young blood around here."

"I'm sorry." Lily set her cards down and crossed her arms at their retired neighbor. "What am I? Chopped liver?"

Ralph chuckled. "Now don't get all girly on me. You know we love you. Why don't you remind the boy how not to tick off his partner before the General pilfers my shillelagh to knock some sense into him?"

It had been years since Jake had heard Ralph tell his stories of working on the commuter trains as a conductor and carrying a small shillelagh to casually thunk troublemakers with. To hear Ralph talk about the good old days, anyone would think the man single handedly saved the railroad from hoodlums and crazy people.

"Go on, now," Ralph urged, winking at Jake.

Hiding a snort of laughter behind a forced cough, Lily turned to him. "You always bleed trump first. Then play your aces, but never sit on your best cards."

"Exactly." The General tapped his folded cards on the table top. "Turn your losers into winners."

"Yes, sir." Jake resisted the urge to salute. When the General had popped by the hardware store a few days ago to pick up a pipe wrench and a snake to unstop a clogged drain in George's absence, Jake hadn't expected the older man to tack on an invitation to play cards. It had been ages since he'd graced the porch of the Hart House during a card game, and though he'd tried as gracefully as possible to take a rain check, somehow by the time the General had left the store, Jake was committed. "Bleed trump," he repeated.

"And don't hold your aces. Remember," the General spouted and Lily mouthed in tandem with him, "rules are rules for a reason."

"Yes, sir." He smothered the urge to smile. Once a military man, always a military man. Even if Jake hadn't grown up with a military grandfather of his own and served for Uncle Sam himself in the Marine Corps, he'd still know that uttering the cliché *rules were meant to be broken* would be enough to give any commanding officer apoplexy. The General was no exception. Gathering the cards, he passed them to his left.

Like her cousin Rose, Lily sported flaming red hair that blossomed from the top of her head in a high ponytail. Her bright green eyes still laughed as the game moved on.

The hum of water pressure kicked up a notch and he turned to Mrs. Hart. "You running the dishwasher or washing machine?"

"Not likely," she laughed. "No, that'll be Heather upstairs. She and Cindy were at the clinic with the animals all afternoon. She's been holed up in that guest room on some super serious phone call since dinner."

"Well," Floyd tapped a card on the table, "that's what happens when you have granddaughters with important careers."

Thelma Carson, owner of the antique store, and a member of the town's unofficial Merry Widows Club, nodded. "That's right. And isn't that a blessing. Poor Meredith LeBlanc. Three adult children and not a single one showing any signs of moving out and growing up."

"Don't you have a diamond?" Floyd asked.

"Of course I do."

"Then why are you playing trump?"

Thelma looked down at her cards. "Oh, well. I guess I got distracted thinking about poor Meredith."

Jake chuckled, raising his cards to hide his laughter.

While the friends chattered back and forth over their cards, he wondered how he'd missed hearing that Heather had come to town. Between her going away to school and his serving in the Marines, he couldn't remember the last time they'd crossed paths. She was the closest to him in age and the one most likely to be off somewhere with her nose in a book. And certainly the only teenager he could think of who would read a biology book for the fun of it.

"Now there's a girl who knows how to keep track of cards played," the General boomed. Somehow, from him even a compliment sounded like a command.

"I bet she does," he agreed. Anyone who could master the art of heart surgery should be able to understand the principles of bidding and playing cards.

Having won the bid and organized his hand, Jake discarded the four unwanted cards. "Hearts are trump."

"Now remember this time, take control of the board." His expression softening, the General leaned over to pat each of his dogs on the head, then sat up, furrowing his brow at Jake. "Otherwise we're switching partners."

"Not on your life," Mrs. Hart teased.

Lily only rolled her eyes.

While debating which card to play first, his ace or a losing trump, a shriek from the second floor jolted him to his feet. Chairs scraped against the wooden porch floor and footsteps pounded behind him. First to reach the foot of the stairs, he noticed the blur of a woman dashing down in his direction.

He'd barely had time to shift to the side to avoid a collision when the feminine form glanced up, screeched to a halt, and blinked away the water clinging to her lashes. Suds still in her damp blonde hair, she swallowed hard, gripping the towel tighter around herself.

Coming to sudden stop, Lily stumbled into him. "What happened?"

The entire group of card players flanked him on the landing.

Heather looked from him to her cousin and then back again. "I don't know."

With an instinctive will of its own, Jake's gaze traveled slowly from the top of her dripping wet hair to the sleek curve of well-shaped calves and delicate ankles.

Hand on her chest, Heather sucked in a calming breath. "The water was getting cold so I went to move the handle for the shower more to the left and it just…well, it fell into my hand. Now steaming hot water is spewing and I can't turn it off."

"Let me take a look." Jake shifted around her, thankful for any excuse to keep his eyes forward, and his hands where they belonged.

"You might need this." She held out the broken faucet handle.

Like a runner in a relay race, he barely paused to grab the contraption as he rushed past her, taking the stairs two at a time he galloped to the gushing bathroom. The last thing he needed was for the General to catch him ogling a half-naked granddaughter. Now all Jake had to do was get the image of droplet covered bare shoulders out of his mind and stop the impending floods. Piece of cake. *Right.*

# CHAPTER THREE

Grabbing the first thing on the top of her bag, Heather stepped into a pair of slacks and pulling on an old sweater, twirled her long, damp hair into a neat bun at the back of her head, carefully pinning any stray strands into submission. Her heart was still pounding hard and fast against her ribs. She could hold a human heart in her hand and stay calm as a cucumber, but let a plumbing fixture fall into those hands and then have her run full speed ahead into a handsome male specimen, and she was more flustered than a virgin bride on her wedding night.

How could she have forgotten there would be a porch full of card players to gather about and view her performance in nothing but her birthday suit and a skimpy towel?

She wasn't sure who was more surprised, her or Jake. Remembering the look on his face when he'd caught sight of her had her heart pounding even faster. The last time she'd seen Jake Harper he'd been a skinny sixteen-year-old tripping over his big feet and waving a shiny new driver's license. Boy, had he ever grown into those feet. She didn't know which was more ridiculous, getting all bent out of shape over flashing half the town or because a deliciously handsome man had nearly swallowed his tongue at the sight of her. Not that he'd done anything stupid, but the way his eyes widened and the muscles in his jaw tightened, she didn't think it had anything to do with old pipes and everything to do with practically crashing into a half naked woman. And as much as her feminine ego would like to think it had something to do with crashing into her, she knew enough about human nature—and anatomy—to know his visceral response would have been the same no matter the woman. *Too bad.*

Just because the entire episode had been the most embarrassing thing to happen to her since she was twelve and lost her bikini top jumping off the Point was no reason to hide out in her room. If her teenage self could recover from a little bare flesh, Dr. Heather Preston could most certainly face the man who had seen more of her skin up close and personal than any other human in close to a decade.

Slowly, she took a deep breath, gripped the doorknob and opened the door just in time to run smack dab into Jake's chest—again. He hit her like a wall of stone.

A bright smile beamed down on her. "We have to stop meeting like this."

Blinking, she shook her head. "Sorry, I wanted to see if you needed any help."

Raking one hand through damp brown hair, brushing it away from his forehead and running the other across his green sweater marked with a few spots of water and grime, he shrugged. "Nothing we can do now. I found the shut off valve. The fixture didn't seem that old, but the valve stems were stripped. Sometimes you get a clunker. They'll need to be replaced. Since George isn't around I'd be happy to fix it for the General."

"You?" She hadn't meant for her surprise to come out more like shock.

The way his one brow shot up to his hairline, he'd noticed too. "The perks of owning a hardware store and having a plumber for a father is I not only have all the parts, I know what to do with them."

She knew he was talking about fixing the shower, but the way he'd phrased his sentence had her mouth growing dry and her wrestling the urge to glance down at his...parts.

Since his expression remained unchanged, either he didn't realize how what he'd said could be misinterpreted, or he chose to ignore it. "If your granddad calls Mike, this will cost him a fortune. Doesn't make sense to pay George a salary and a plumber on top of that."

"Still, you have your own business to run. Responsibilities. I'm sure we can figure—"

He raised a finger in the air. "Your grandparents are always volunteering Hart House and the lakefront any time the community needs a fundraiser or celebration. They do more than their share for the folks in this town. I don't mind giving back. It's the perks of having a good relationship with my boss. I know he won't fire me." Jake flashed a grin that could make most girls weak in the knees.

Including her.

"Thank you."

Waving his arm away, he waited for her to start down the stairs. "How long will you be in town?"

Unfortunately, she didn't own her own hospital, so just walking away when her grandparents needed help wasn't an option. "Just till Sunday night." She refrained from mentioning her ulterior motives—for now. Cindy hadn't noticed any signs of trouble and promised to keep an extra eye out. And Heather had left a message at her grandfather's doctor's office this afternoon. If she didn't hear back from the man soon, she might be telling a lot more people why she was here.

"Heather?" Lily's voice broke through her thoughts "Oh, Jake, are you all finished?"

"Yeah," Jake nodded. "But no one should use this bathroom until I can get back tomorrow and finish it right."

"Not a problem, Heather is the only who uses this bathroom when she visits, and besides, it's not like there aren't enough bathrooms in this big old place." Lily smiled and turned to her cousin. "Do you have more important calls to make or will you be joining us outside?"

"Pot calling the kettle black, Miss Cordon Blue Bakery Chef," Heather teased.

Lifting her chin with an air of sophistication and a hint of a French accent, Lily corrected her cousin, "Not bakery, darling, Patisserie," then cracked up laughing. "Really, the General and Grams are calling it a night. Cindy, Poppy and Callie are on their way. Since you won't be staying after supper Sunday, Cindy suggested it's a perfect night for one of our bonfires on the beach."

"I do need to talk to you guys, but it's getting late. I've had a stack of journals to catch up on and this would be—"

"Heather." Lily hoisted her hands on to her hips. "It's the lake."

Staying on top of her game, top of her field, meant she spent almost as much time curled up with medical journals as she did in the OR. It really had been too long since Heather had spent more than a few hours at the lake, and even on those occasions her head had always been somewhere else, mentally planning the next complex surgery.

"You should go." Jake smiled down at her. "Bonfires by the lake, even at our age, are still cool."

"That's right." Lily bobbed her head. "And you should join us too, Jake."

"Don't bakers have to get up at some insane hour of the morning?" Heather asked.

"We do. And I'm still going to the beach."

Lily always had been the one who could talk a starving man into giving up a meal.

"What do you say, Doc?" Jake lifted his hands palms up. "I'm game if you are?"

Even as her mind thought no, her head nodded yes, and her mouth muttered *sure*. Meanwhile, she still didn't know a thing more about her grandfather's health than when she'd spoken to him on the phone two days ago. Her to-be-read pile wouldn't be getting shorter any time soon, and without a broken fixture in sight, her heart was once again banging anxiously against her breast bone. What was that all about?

● ● ● ●

Already waiting at the water's edge, two of the three women huddled around a growing fire on the beach shot up and rushed toward Heather. Jake recognized the cousins and smiled. Anyone watching would have thought they hadn't seen Heather in years rather than months.

There wasn't anything unusual about Jake running into one of the four sisters here in town. Like their mom Virginia, Callie the high school gym teacher, Poppy the bookkeeper, Cindy the veterinarian, and of course Lily the best baker the Hilltop Inn had ever had, all lived in town. Still, it was odd for him to see so many of the Hart granddaughters in one place at one time.

While the cousins hugged and giggled, Cindy sat quietly poking at the fire, and Lily reached into a cooler and held a drink up to Jake.

He shook his head, mouthing no thanks, and Lily wandered over to sit beside Cindy.

"Finally." Callie stepped back. "I couldn't believe you'd actually show up until I saw you for myself."

"Relax." Heather hugged Poppy, the youngest of the four sisters, but answered Callie. "I'm just visiting. I'm not dying."

"I know, but when was the last time you spent more than a few hours at the lake?" Reaching behind her head, Callie undid her hair, stuck a big toothy clip between her teeth, twirled the golden ponytail into a sloppy bun, and clipped it all back in place atop her head. "And even then you barely have time to eat and run, never mind actually sit and chat. You're impossible to reach on the phone and trying to get updates from Rose or Violet on your life isn't any better. Apparently even though the three of you live in the same city, you don't spend any more time with them than you do here at the lake. Tell us, what is new and exciting in your bustling life?"

Heather took a seat by the fire. "There's nothing much to tell. I've been doing the same thing since med school. Work, work, and more work."

"Yeah." Poppy, the only cousin dressed in a long flowy skirt, eased onto the sand by her sister, shooting a sweet smile at her cousin. "Busy saving lives."

A glint of pride shone in Heather's eyes as each of her cousins smiled.

Once the girls took their places at the fire, Jake found himself dropping into the only empty spot left between Heather and Cindy. Not a bad seat.

"Enough of the mushy stuff." Cindy looked up from the fire. "We need to get some business out of the way."

Heather nodded. This was after all the reason she'd come to the lake.

Lily and her other sisters sported identical frowns of confusion.

"Perhaps, I should double check that leaky pipe?" Even though they'd barely just sat down, Jake leaned forward to push to his feet. "Enough of the mushy stuff." Cindy looked up from the fire. "We need to get some business out of the way."

Heather nodded. This was after all the reason she'd come to the lake.

Lily and her other sisters sported identical frowns of confusion.

Shaking her head, Heather reached out and grabbed his arm. "Please stay."

He must have hesitated, because Cindy nodded at him as well then waited for him to sit back down before starting. "Have any of you noticed anything different about the General?"

"Different how?" Poppy inched forward.

"Sick different," Heather volunteered.

Three heads, plus Jake's, whipped around to face her.

Callie heaved a deep sigh. "How sick?"

"This is why you're here on a Wednesday night." Poppy looked ready to burst into tears.

"Yes." Heather nodded at Poppy then turned to Callie. "I don't know how sick."

Lily twisted around to face Cindy. "How much do you know?"

Holding both her hands up, Cindy shook her head. "Only what Heather told me this afternoon."

"Which is?" Callie asked.

Heather repeated the concerns she'd already shared with Cindy, her brief medical observations since arriving at her grandfather's, and the struggle she was having getting any information from the General or his doctor. Not that Jake expected Old Doc Wilkins to break doctor patient privilege, but for some reason he thought doctor to doctor the man might have been more willing to assuage Heather's concerns.

"So you're here because of a cough?" Poppy blinked.

Heather nodded.

"And you saw him lose his balance?" Callie chimed in.

Heather sighed. "Don't forget he's lost some weight too."

"All of which can be signs of something more serious." Cindy tossed some leaves into the fire.

"I don't know." Lily shook her head. "He hasn't lost that much weight, and I can't say that I've noticed anything different about him. We played cards tonight and I don't remember hearing him cough even once." She turned to Jake, waited for him to shake his head in confirmation. "But, I say we err on the side of caution. I'll hog tie him, Cindy can throw him in the trunk and Callie can keep Lady and Sarge at bay."

"Don't I get a job?" Poppy actually looked hurt not to be

included in the ludicrous quip.

If Jake didn't know Lily so well, he would never have noticed the concern in her eyes as she teased her sisters. "You," Lily smiled, "get to keep Grams from setting him free."

Nodding briskly and leaning back on her elbows, the thin smile across Poppy's face said she was pleased with her task.

"I would pay some big bucks to see that scenario play out." He smiled. "I can't picture a SEAL team hog-tying the General, never mind four of his granddaughters."

"I don't want to lose him." Ignoring his comment, Poppy pulled her knees up to her chin and draped her arms around her legs, tugging her skirt down over her toes.

He knew exactly how she felt. Everything about this place, including the General, was an anchor of sorts. As kids, everyone knew everyone, and hanging out on the Point at Hart House was the place to be. The land had been in the Hart family since the days of the revolution. During the depression, the General's grandfather built several small cottages along the sloping landscape and rented them out to the few wealthy people who could afford to get away from the city and commune with nature. About the same time, the General's father and grandfather had built a stone pier into the lake, at least forty feet wide and seventy-five feet long with grassy fill for game playing or sun bathing. Nestled between the creek and the beach and affectionately referred to as the Point, it was prime real estate for adults and kids alike. He'd learned to pitch horseshoes and knock a croquet ball around on that swath of manmade land.

Like the movie *The Sandlot*, as kids grew up, went to college, to work, got married or started families, the weekends at the lake saw fewer of the familiar families and instead grew crowded with cottage guests and new summer tourists. But there was still the occasional card game on the porch, charity fundraisers, summer holiday barbecues with half the town watching the Fourth of July fireworks on the lake, and since his retirement, there was always the General.

"Can't you just give the General a checkup?" Poppy asked.

All heads turned to face the pretty brunette.

"Never mind." She shook her head almost laughing and waving a thumb at Jake. "Like the man said, what was I thinking?"

"She's right, though," Cindy said. "We have to do something and Heather is the most qualified."

"I'm willing to give it another day before I do anything. But we all need to observe the General. Carefully. Look for anything out of the usual."

"Like?" Lily asked.

"How much is he drinking? Is he always thirsty?"

"Diabetes," Cindy offered.

"What does that have to do with coughing?" Poppy shifted to sit cross legged, tucking her skirt carefully over her knees.

"It doesn't," Lily added. "What are you really worried about?"

"Heart disease."

The glow of the fire highlighted the concern etched on all the women's faces. Even thin lipped and frowning, there wasn't an ugly one in the bunch. Now that he thought about it, all of the cousins were knockouts as teens. He suspected even the cousins like Heather, who he hadn't seen in years, were probably still turning heads.

"I'll keep an extra eye on him too," Jake tossed in. "I have to come back tomorrow. I can ask him to help me."

"The General?" Heather asked wide-eyed. "The man is allergic to tools. He had an entire Marine Corps at his disposal for that sort of thing."

"And now he has George," Cindy added.

"But he likes to oversee. The last few weeks, whenever I deliver supplies for his daughter's current remodel—"

"That would be my mother." Heather raised her hand and waved a finger.

Jake nodded. "Without fail, if the General wasn't standing over us double checking the deliveries, he wasn't far away watching. My mom's dad was a Commander in the Navy. He had his favorite stories. One he often retold included an aircraft carrier, a special forces team, a brawl, and the Marines' commanding officer—old Eagle Eye Hart. It was years later before I figured out Eagle Eye and your grandfather were one and the same. " Jake smiled at Heather. "Give me a list of things to look for.

Heather nodded and he thought he saw some of the tension ease from her shoulders. He really did want to help.

"Now that we have a plan for the General," Lily rubbed her hands together, "I want to hear everything I've missed the last few months."

Heather shrugged.

"There must be something fun in your life. Handsome doctors? Quiet dinners in dimly lit restaurants?"

"What are you, a baker or a romance author?" Heather looked at her cousin as though she'd sprouted a third boob.

"Do we have to drag information out of you like when we were ten?" Callie laughed.

"Oh, yes." Jake chuckled. "Truth or dare." From what he remembered from his summer shenanigans on the Point with the Hart granddaughters, from a very early age, Heather was the serious one who on the odd occasion they could convince her to join them always, always chose truth. Unlike him, who would rather do a dare any day of the week.

Heather rolled her eyes. "Oh, for land sakes. We don't need to play games. I haven't been on a date in years. Unless you count coffee in the cafeteria with a near retiring anesthesiologist with grandchildren a date, I don't have a clue what romance is. Even if Prince Charming pulled up on his white steed to whisk me away, I'd probably have to say no because I need to be at the hospital at five in the morning to prep for surgery."

This time the other cousins groaned and Lily leaned back laughing. "Don't we make for boring gossip?"

None of this was boring for Jake; he was thoroughly enjoying himself. Watching the girls interact. Watching Heather. From all he'd seen and heard tonight, the young bookworm had turned into one incredible butterfly. Of course, after this little impromptu lakeside visit, he probably wouldn't see her again for another decade or so. And wasn't that a shame.

# CHAPTER FOUR

"Uh oh." Staring down at the pile of goods in front of him, Tom followed his words with a tsk-tsk sound.

Jake didn't bother to look up. Once the usual morning rush of contractors had come and gone, he'd needed to finish off some accounting and receiving records before heading out to do a few odd jobs. The problem was his ins and outs were jumbling up with his credits and debits and he didn't want to even think about what he'd done with shipping and receiving. The only clear thing in his mind was Heather. Heather dripping wet, Heather barely dry, Heather blushing at his accidental double entendre and Heather in the glow of the firelight.

"Since this isn't in the shipping area, am I correct that this is more pro bono work?"

"Yes." Jake pushed away from his desk before he made a bigger mess of the paperwork. Tom had been right about Mrs. Norton. Some of the wood siding was in desperate need of replacing before winter set in. It wouldn't take Jake very long to make the repairs and then he could head over to the General's to fix the shower handle. Not that Mike the plumber wouldn't have been willing to help the General out in George's absence the same as he was, but he liked having a good reason to spend a little more time with the Harts. Especially the one stuck in his mind.

"You do know that the main purpose of a store is to sell." Tom helped him carry the cement siding to the back of the delivery truck.

"Do unto others..." Jake added screws and caulk to the pile. Tom was just as likely to help out as he was. After all, it was Tom who suggested Jake take a closer look at the Norton place.

Chuckling under his breath, Tom shook his head. "Need help?"

No surprise that Tom had come around to volunteering. "Not this time. Thanks."

"Anyone home?" a voice called out from the front of the shop.

Jake recognized the voice and straightening, slapped Tom on the back. "Load the rest of this stuff, please. I'll take care of the customer."

"There you are," the General enunciated loud and clear as though addressing one of his underlings.

"Twice in one week," Jake teased. He couldn't remember, before this week, the last time the General had wandered through the store.

"Dropped my Fiona off at the Hilltop Inn for one of those ladies art league lunches she so loves. Thought I'd come by and thank you again for helping out last night."

"Of course. Glad I was there." Though, he'd had enough conversation with the General over construction supplies and remodels to know darn well that the old guy could turn a shut off valve.

"Probably should take one of your homeowner classes in case anything like this happens again."

"Oh, if you want to, sure." At this stage of life if the old man wanted to learn how to wield the new wrench he'd bought, who was Jake to argue. "I'll let you know when the next plumbing class is scheduled."

"Very well." The General clicked his heels and stepped back. "I'm heading across the street for a bite to eat. Care to join me?"

All set to say thanks but he had a few things to do before heading to Hart House to work on the shower, Jake remembered his promise to Heather. How better to get info out of the old man than over a leisurely lunch. "Sounds great."

The door chimed and a windswept Heather stormed into the store. Her timing worthy of a well-scripted movie. Determination oozing from every pore, the woman was definitely on a mission. Quickly scanning the front of the store, her gaze landed on her grandfather. "Mrs. Franklin said I'd find you here."

The General frowned. "And why, may I ask, are you looking for me?"

"You agreed you'd call Dr. Wilkins this morning. By the time I came downstairs from showering and dressing, you were gone."

And wasn't that an image Jake didn't need added to his playlist.

"I had to drive your grandmother into town."

"Yes, that's what Lucy said."

"Then why are you talking with that old busy body Mrs. Franklin?"

Heather's back teeth clenched tight before she blew out a short breath and slowly enunciated. "Because you weren't at the barber shop, or the cigar shop—"

"Gave those up."

Heather frowned, missing a beat. "When was that?"

"Don't remember," the General shrugged.

The way Heather stared him down before saying another word told Jake she didn't believe he'd forgotten any more than Jake did. Anyone who could keep track of cards dealt and discarded with the precision the General did, would know exactly when he'd given up cigars.

"Anyhow," Heather continued, "I would like it if you would please call to authorize—"

"Not now. Jake and I are just heading across the street for a bite to eat. Since you're here you can join us."

"But Doc Wilkins is…"

There was no point in finishing the sentence. The General was halfway out the door.

"Well, you wanted to keep an eye on him." Jake waved an arm toward the front door. "Here's our chance."

"Yes. Isn't it." Through a plastic smile, Heather sucked in a long deep breath and blew it out slowly on her first brisk step forward. "Just peachy keen."

Jake had to laugh to himself. Apparently Dr. Heather Preston had a thing or two to learn about going with the flow. As for himself, he was really starting to like the way things were *flowing* around here. Yes, sir. Just peachy keen.

• • • •

The neon pink sign flickering open in the window of Mabel's Diner was almost a town icon. Mabel's sour cream blueberry pie was the holy grail. Many a tourist made the pilgrimage to see and taste their town treasures, and today was clearly one of those days. The place was packed and it was barely a few minutes past eleven.

"Sorry." Martha, Mabel's eldest daughter, came running up to them. "We had a tour bus come through late. I'll get you a table for two."

"Three," Jake and Heather echoed. Martha looked over their shoulder.

"My grandfather." Heather pointed behind Martha to the General chatting up a table across the way.

"I don't have a table for three just yet." Martha smiled and spun around, scanning the crowded tables from one end of the diner to the other. "It might be a bit. If you'll have a seat on the bench out—"

"Tell you what," Jake waved a hand at Martha and flashed a reassuring grin, "I need to drop something off at Floyd's. What if I go do that and then we come back?"

Relief deflated Martha's lungs in a single whoosh. "Oh, that would be great. Once this bus is gone we'll have plenty of room."

"Sounds like a plan." Holding the glass door open with an extended arm, Jake ushered Heather out the door. "Looks like we've got a few minutes to kill."

"What about Floyd's?"

"Just an excuse to make Martha feel better. Mabel takes crowds and folks waiting in stride. Not that she doesn't do her best to accommodate everyone as quickly as possible, but Martha still flusters pretty easy when the place is at capacity."

Heather fell into step beside Jake. Walking casually past Betty's Cut and Set, she had a feeling he'd shortened his stride to match hers. "I thought I remember Grams mentioning Betty sold the salon."

"She did." He smiled. "To Elizabeth Barker. Originally she'd intended to go into business in the suburbs, but when she and her family came to town for vacation and she spotted Betty's for sale, well," he shrugged, "she considered it fate."

This morning Heather had been in such a rush to find her grandfather and drag him to the doctor, she hadn't really looked around town. "Things haven't changed much, have they?"

"The town is a bit bigger, but for the most part things stay the same around here. It's one of the things I love about it."

"I would think the star of the football team and the guy probably every girl wanted to take her to prom would have been itching to move away. You know, spread your wings in the big city."

"Nope." Jake shook his head. "I might have felt that way in high school, but after giving Uncle Sam six years of my life, a good number of them served in the sand box—"

"Sand box?"

"Afghanistan and Iraq, that part of the world. There's a lot of desert."

An article she'd read once about emergency heart surgery in-country before shuttling the patient to Germany came to mind. One of the interviewees had referred to the sand box.

"Anyhow," he pointed to the Village Creamery and the bistro tables set up along the narrow sidewalk, "there wasn't a day when I was away that I didn't dream of Millie's homemade butter pecan ice cream with a dollop of hand whipped cream, or Mabel's blueberry pie, or the occasional single blade hand shave at Floyds, or just about everyone else in this town. Lawford is the only place I ever want to live."

For the first time in a long time she took in the length of Main Street. The colorful signs. The mostly shiplap buildings. The few people milling about. The memories from childhood filtering to the front of her thoughts. The Creamery had always been a treat. For her it was Vanilla ice cream with marshmallow topping.

They strolled past Floyds, the barber shop where her grandfather and his cronies still played checkers a few days a week. For as long as the Harts and the Lawfords had lived on this mountain, the red and white candy-striped pole had spun outside the small storefront. Though unlike Elizabeth who kept the shop's name because it was a version of her own, Floyd had bought the shop that sported the same name as a TV classic back before her mom and aunts had married, kept the business name and used it as his own.

"The summer I was in kindergarten," Heather paused, looking up the old barber post, "my grandfather would bring me with him and let me play checkers on his lap. He'd told me the story of the barber shop and how everyone in town continued to call the new barber Floyd even though that wasn't his name."

"As a kid I'd seen reruns of the Andy Griffith show and assumed all barbers were named Floyd." Jake chuckled, his gaze following the swirling stripes upward.

Heather laughed, wondering what childhood memories this spot brought back for him. No matter how often she'd asked her grandfather about Floyd, to this day, she still didn't know what the barber's real name was. "Do *you* know his real name?"

"Nope."

Looking over her shoulder she caught Floyd's attention through the picture frame window. His face lit up and a pair of scissors in one hand, he waved at her with the other. At the same moment, seated at the small round table along the wall, checker piece in hand, Ralph glanced up and smiled. For the first time in days, thoughts of Kyle, the hospital, and surgery took a backseat to the peace and tranquility of the lakeside Main Street.

At her side, Jake waved at both men. "Yep. No place else." Lacing his hand around her waist, he nudged her to turn in place. "There goes the bus. We can catch up with the General now."

The moment they opened the diner door, Martha came running up to them. "Perfect timing. Follow me." She hurried to a nice booth near the back of the diner and smiled at Heather. "It's been a while since you've been by. It's really nice to see you."

Considering Heather couldn't remember the last time she'd been here, she wasn't sure why Martha remembered her at all. "It's nice to be back." The truth was, despite the circumstances, it really was nice. In only twenty-four hours, she already felt more relaxed and rested than she has since the summer before med school.

"Guess it's hard to get away from the city, you working so hard and all." Martha handed them each a menu and stepped back. "Mom—I mean Mabel—will be by to take your order shortly."

Heather nodded.

"Ned Baker better get those hearing aids of his checked. Damn hard to keep up a conversation when every other word out of his mouth is *whatcha say*." The General slid into the booth beside Heather. "I'm so hungry I could eat a buffalo."

"What did you have for breakfast?" Heather asked.

The General shook his head. "No time."

"How long have you been sleeping in?"

"Oh look." The General slid out of the seat. "Pete Stephens just came in. I've been trying to nail that man down for almost two weeks now. Man wants to spend our tax dollars to install speakers on Main Street. We'll just see about that." And he was off.

"General," Heather reached for her grandfather, but the man was more slippery than a greased eel.

Jake kept an eye on the old man's departing back. "Do you suppose he really cares about speakers on Main Street?"

"What I think," Heather twisted around to face Jake, "is that he doesn't want me peppering him with any more questions."

"Still worried?"

Was she? Lily had been right, since her arrival yesterday she hadn't heard her grandfather cough once, nor had she seen him lose his balance. "He's sleeping late."

Jake studied her a moment. "Anemia?"

"Could be, but I'm still thinking cardiac issues. If you've got a clogged valve, not enough oxygen is getting to your brain and other organs—"

"And you get tired and might sleep in. Got it."

"Or," Heather toyed with her fork, "he's simply taking life easy for once and I'm making a mountain out of the proverbial mole hill."

"You didn't make up the cough or the dizziness."

"No, no I didn't." And just like that, years of medical training kicked in and took front seat once again in her mind.

"Well aren't you a sight for sore eyes." Mabel leaned over to hug Heather. "As a welcome home and glad to see you, one slice of pie on the house."

"Uh hmm," Jake cleared his throat.

"Sorry, friend," Mabel chuckled softly. "You I see all the time."

"Can't blame a man for trying." He grinned up at her.

Mabel smiled at him and looked to Heather. "What'll you have?"

"I'll stick with the tried and true. Grilled chicken Caesar salad and a diet pop."

"The usual for you?" Mabel asked Jake.

"Yep."

"One swiss bacon and mushroom cheese burger with extra fries and mayo on the side for you, and a grilled chicken sandwich and a side of fruit for the General."

"I'm sorry." Heather set her menu down and stared up at Mabel. "Did you say my grandfather ordered a grilled chicken sandwich?"

"That's right. Been his regular order the last few times he's been in."

Before Heather could say another word, Mabel had turned and scurried toward the kitchen.

Heather cast her gaze on Jake. "I have never, ever in my life known the General to come into Mabel's and order anything besides her fried chicken with french fries and a side of creamed corn. The artery clogging special."

"Maybe it doesn't mean anything?" Jake's gaze skipped over to the General and back.

"Right," Heather tsked. "And my cousins and I are not the product of three wanna-be hippie sisters who named all of their daughters after flowers. "

"Well, the flower part may be true, but I'm not sure about your grandfather. I mean, Louise Franklin has been working at the pharmacy for as long as I can remember and that woman has never been able to keep a secret."

"And your point?"

"If your grandfather were seriously ill, though she can't come right out and say so, you'd better believe she would be fawning and fussing over your grandmother, organizing church pot luck suppers and who knows what else to," he made a pair of air quotes, "help."

"I don't know." She took a sip of the water Mabel had set on the table.

A twinkle in his eyes, he cocked his head at her. "Have you really forgotten how small towns work?"

Had she? The last time she'd spent any length of time at the lake she was a boring senior in high school. A far cry from the little girl who sat on her grandfather's lap playing checkers. She sat back in her seat, took in Jake's charming grin, the twinkle in his eye that reminded her of a man walking down memory lane, and smiled herself. "You got caught."

He had the decency to blush. "Often."

"And to think last night my sisters were squeezing me for gossip.

Do tell."

"Nothing that interesting. Kid stuff." He shrugged. "It was a long time ago."

Heather shook her head. "No sir. Copouts unacceptable. Shall I guess?"

"Go for it." Jake folded strong arms across his chest.

The man had to work out for arms like that.

"Heather?"

"Oh sorry." She studied him a moment pulling her mind away from how the guy would look great on the cover of a novel wearing a buttoned down tux with a tie hanging loosely around his neck. "At least one story has to involve Mrs. Franklin."

Jake gave her a lazy one shoulder shrug.

"Definitely Mrs. Franklin. She caught you with a girl."

The tips of his ears singed slightly and she knew she was on the right track. Without her saying a word, the rosy tone was covering his ears and working its way down his cheeks.

"Oh my. She caught you in *the* act, so to speak."

Jake twirled the straw wrapper in his fingers.

"Someone I know?" This was getting interesting.

Shaking his head, Jake leaned back. "Sorry. A summer tourist."

Momentarily deflated at guessing wrong, Heather perked up. "But I was right about everything else."

"Almost everything else. I was as close to a homerun as I'd ever come when Mrs. Franklin decided a pre-dawn stroll by the point was the perfect cure for insomnia."

"Our Point?" She had to blink to keep her eyes from popping.

"Nah. The General was in country then. The abandoned point by the old marina. My mother never let me live that down."

"Ouch."

"Yeah, but it was worse when I borrowed my dad's car to make a beer run across the lake."

"Dare I ask how old you were?"

Jake shook his head. "You probably don't want to hear about skinny dipping with your cousin Lily?"

This time her eyes really burst open wide. "You went skinny dipping with Lily?"

"Not exactly with. She coaxed the football team into it and somehow she managed to be the only one not in the water and I wound up her accomplice in hiding their clothes. To this day I'm still not sure how we were found out."

"But you were?"

"For the next six months, every time my mom walked away from me she always shook her head."

"And your dad?"

"I think he thought most of it, except for the incident with the townie, was funny and managed to put on a good front with Mom."

They went silent as Mabel came by and set their food on the table.

"What about my grandfather's lunch?" Heather asked

Mabel pointed across the way. "He's eating with Pete Stephens. Anything else?"

Heather and Jake shook their heads.

"So what about you?" Jake lifted a french fry. "Any youthful indiscretions?"

Stabbing at her salad, Heather shook her head. "Not a single indiscretion, youthful or otherwise."

"Nose in a book."

"Excuse me?"

"You always had your nose in a book."

"I had a goal. From the time I was rather young I knew I wanted to be a doctor. By the time I hit junior high I understood how much work it would take to get there."

"A girl with a plan."

"A meticulous plan. Followed it every step of the way. Right up to working as a fellow and now along side the best chief of cardiothoracic surgery in the country in one of the most prestigious hospitals on the Eastern seaboard."

"And you love every minute of it. It's written all over your face."

"I love my work. More than anything." She glanced across the restaurant. Her concern for her grandfather gurgled to the surface. The truth was as much as she loved what she did, she'd give it up in a heartbeat for the people who meant the most to her. She just hoped that day never came.

# CHAPTER FIVE

"Jake, what a pleasant surprise." Sadie Norton opened the front door. "Are you here to check the sink?"

"Actually," he glanced over her shoulder and hoped little white lies weren't going to count in the after-life, "I've got these leftover pieces of siding that I can't sell." Mostly because he'd sawed them in half before leaving the shop. "Noticed you have a few rotten boards and if you wouldn't mind, it would help me make room for new product if I could just give them to you."

The way her brows formed the perfect scowl, he was pretty sure she was either about to call him out for the liar he was, or debating if she could manage to hammer the things up herself. "I want to help, but—"

"Great. I brought my tool box. If you'll give me about an hour, I'll have the old boards down and the new ones in place." He took a step back and hurried away before she could object.

What he hadn't counted on was her scurrying after him. "Now just a minute. You said leave here, you didn't say a word about installation."

Jake came to a screeching halt. Thinking fast, he looked down to his feet before slowly lifting his chin and smiling at the woman. "You caught me."

"Caught you?" Her brows unbuckled and lifted high with curiosity.

"I was hoping I could keep some of the bad wood for kindling."

"Oh." She took a step back, her expression brightening. "Well, I suppose that would be a fair exchange. But you'll have to let me sweeten the deal."

"Yes, ma'am." What was one more frozen beef stew dinner?

"It'll take me more than an hour, but I was just about to bake some of my apple pies for the church bazaar. I'll see to it you get one free of charge. Folks fight over my apple pies. Best in the county.

Always take the prize at the fair."

"Yes ma'am." He smiled. Mission accomplished.

He'd barely lifted the first boards out of his truck when he recognized the two door coupe with Massachusetts plates pulling up to the curb.

"I thought that was you." Heather slid out of her car, easing her sunglasses away from her face and smiling up at him. Even though he'd left her trying to corral her grandfather little more than an hour ago, her bright grin hit him with the same force as a sucker punch from a giant. So far in the last twenty-four hours he'd seen her in varying stages of dress, undress, and social repartee. What he hadn't seen until now was a deep down grin with a halo of sunlight bouncing off her blonde hair.

When she'd come into the shop looking for her grandfather earlier this morning, she'd had her hair neatly pinned back like a turn of the century—the last century—schoolmarm. Now she'd let it loose to cascade around her shoulders and he had to make every effort not to swallow his tongue. He was never going to get to sleep tonight.

"Gave up on my grandfather and was heading back to the house." Waving a thumb over her shoulder in the general direction up the road, she took a step forward. "Thought for sure you'd beat me there."

He resisted the urge—for his own good—to take a step back. "Had to make this one stop first."

Her gaze shifted from him to the boards he'd set down on the bed of his truck over to the house. "A man of many talents."

If there had been any saliva left in his mouth he would have swallowed hard; as it was the best he could manage was a nod.

"Need any help?"

Okay, not what he'd expected to hear. "You do carpentry?"

She chuckled and the throaty rumble brought a smile to his face. "Not exactly."

"What does exactly mean?"

"I know what a hammer is." She flashed a toothy grin. "Does that help?"

This time he chuckled loudly. "I suppose you could be the hardware equivalent of a surgical nurse."

"See." She peeled her glasses from atop her head and slid them into a back pocket. "Where do we start? I'm all yours. "

Oh. *So* not the thing to have said. He'd just regained the ability to think and speak and she tossed a line like that at him. Talk about lethal weapons. Sucking in a deep breath and blowing it out slow enough to gather his wits, but not so slowly that she'd notice, he pointed to the tool box. "Know what a crow bar is?"

She glanced in the same direction and nodded.

"Good." He lifted the boards from the bed again. "Grab it and follow me."

As he ripped the old boards off the house, Heather retrieved the larger chunks and carried them over to the truck. His extra pair of work gloves slid off her delicate hands from time to time. The last thing he needed was for her to injure herself. He was no idiot. Like a concert pianist, a good surgeon's hands could be magic.

"Well, my my. Is that you, Heather Preston?" Mrs. Norton came hurrying out the door. "I saw you working from my kitchen window. Thought you looked familiar and then it hit me. How are you?"

The woman had pulled her into such a tight hug that Jake actually thought he heard the air woosh from her lungs.

"Fine," she muttered, "and yourself?"

"Oh, well, you know." The older woman who Jake guessed was at least eighty if she was a day, inched back. "One day at a time." The momentary look of melancholy slid away, replaced by a smile. "I'd better get my two workers a refreshing cup of lemonade."

Before either of them could respond, the woman had hurried off, flung open the screen door, and marched herself inside.

"A woman with a mission," Heather muttered.

"I think she misses having someone to fuss over."

Heather nodded. "I vaguely remember hearing Grams mention Mr. Norton passing not long ago, but I hadn't given it much thought. She doesn't have a lot of family around here."

Jake shook his head. There were plenty of old folks like that in town. Grown kids moved to the bigger cities, or out of state, and no one besides the church ladies to keep an eye on them. It was one of the reasons he'd stepped up to help. He'd lost his dad's parents years ago while he was still deployed, but his mom's parents lived in

Virginia where his grandmother had put down roots once his mom was old enough to start school. He'd like to think if they needed help, someone closer to home would step up. In his own way, doing for the seniors in Lawford was like doing for his grandparents.

Together, he and Heather fell into an easy working rhythm, she mostly watching at the ready with a nail or other needed tool. The conversation was light, the smiles frequent.

As a teen, Heather had spent so much time in her books, he'd never gotten a real feel for her. He knew she was serious about wanting to be a doctor, but he hadn't had a clue what had motivated her to work so hard. "When did you first know you wanted to be a doctor?"

"I was nine." Heather bent to pick up another few screws and handed them to him. "Everything about my mother was so very perfect. I never remember her with a single hair out of place. Ever. Her wardrobe was always crisp and pristine and perfect down to the last thread. Dad's work involved an awful lot of dinner parties."

Jake leaned back and waited for the reels in his mind to play out. "Was your dad the one with the vineyard or the banker?"

"Banker. Aunt Marissa married the winemaker."

He turned back to the siding. "Makes sense. In a world like that the concept of the hostess with the mostest still applies."

"Definitely. Mom's table settings could've been photographed for Emily Post. I doubt the Queen of England has more silverware than Mom."

Jake chuckled. Never had he considered the Queen's silver, and now he had visions of forks and spoons dancing in a massive ballroom like a scene from an animated movie.

"Memories of that night are as clear as a high definition program. Even now, knowing all that I know, I can still feel the fright."

He paused his hammer, waiting for what came next.

"I wasn't supposed to be out of bed, so I stayed very quiet. Maybe I already had good instincts at nine, but I noticed one of the guests right away. Something about him seemed off. Of course, now I realize he was sweating profusely. Kept wiping his forehead with his handkerchief. Every so often he'd cough into the same handkerchief and between those symptoms he repeatedly flexed the fingers on his left hand. It actually amazes me now that of all the people at the party not a single one noticed he was in distress."

"Heart attack?"

She nodded.

"No wonder your grandfather coughing has you so alarmed."

Mid extension to hand him another nail, Heather froze. Was that it? A lot of years and life had passed since her parents' friend had had the massive heart attack in her living room with no one in the room knowing how to save him. Guests were screaming and rushing about. Her very calm and together mother became frantic, screaming into the telephone for help. Her father shouted orders, seeking out anyone with some knowledge of CPR, finally hurrying to their neighbor's.

She'd been watching a man die and didn't like it. She didn't think about it often, but it had to be in the back of her mind. Maybe Jake was right. Maybe that's why hearing the General coughing, combined with his age, had caused an irrational sense of panic that had brought her tearing to the lake.

"I don't know," she answered softly. "I do know when our neighbor Dr. Crosby came rushing over the entire mood in the room shifted. She knew exactly what to do. The orders she spouted made a difference. She showed Dad how to do compressions. Blew air into the stricken man's lungs. Used her bag of tricks and training to keep him alive until the EMTs arrived. "

"And that's when you knew." Jake stepped down off the ladder.

She nodded.

"I'd never heard that story before."

Probably because she'd never told anyone else that she'd been hiding at the top of the stairs watching the entire scenario unfold. Not even her sisters. So what was it about this man that had her so easily sharing her only true secret?

● ● ● ●

"And what has you so befuddled?" Grams sat in one of the many large rockers that graced the massive porch. Dressed in a pair of flared pants the woman had probably owned since before Heather was born, along with a bright patchwork quilt top that bore more resemblance to a blanket than a blouse, her grandmother looked up from the clacking needles.

"Life." She lifted her chin, pointing at the yarn in Gram's lap. "Whatcha making?"

"It started out as a scarf for your grandfather," she held up the unbalanced swatch, "but somehow it got away from me, so now it's going to be a baby blanket for the church bazaar."

For as long as Heather could remember, her grandmother looked like she'd be more at home in an artist colony in New Mexico than at a lakeside cottage in New England, and absolutely nothing gave any inkling that she'd once been one of the Lawfords. As in Lawford Mountain and Lawford Granite Quarry. "I'm sure it's going to be as beautiful as you are."

Grams blushed, shook her head, and tsked at her eldest granddaughter. "Flattery will get you everywhere. What would you like?"

Without any thought, Heather sprang forward and pulled her grandmother into a tight embrace.

"Well, now." The aging woman soothed her granddaughter's back with steady strokes. "Usually Poppy is the sentimental one. Or your sister Violet when she's not in a trance."

Heather chuckled and pulled away. "I think you mean meditating."

"If you say so, dear." The woman shrugged and returned to the project in her lap.

Lucy the housekeeper and cook, more family than employee and the town's self-appointed matchmaker, came out humming "Hello Dolly" from one of her favorite musicals and carrying a small tray with two glasses of lemonade. "Thought you might like to join Ms. Fiona for a little refreshment."

To her right, her grandmother already had a full glass on the small table beside her. "I must look thirsty."

Lucy let out a belly laugh that could make a grouch smile. "That's for Jake. He just came through the back door and is upstairs working on the shower plumbing."

"Oh." She tried not to let her glance lift to the second floor, but she realized what she was doing too late. If she didn't watch her step, Lucy would have them volunteering side by side on some committee or worse, like she'd tried a few years ago with Ralph's granddaughter and the then new banker in town, and "accidentally" lock them in the storage shed.

Now Lucy's deep laughter transformed to a smug grin. "Good looking fellow, that young man. Nice too. Those are hard to come by."

Keeping her mouth shut and nodding struck Heather as her best option if she didn't want to find herself trapped in close quarters with an unsuspecting man. Of course the idea of getting up close and personal with Jake held more appeal than it should; she had patients to get back to. No matter how she might reply, she knew that somehow, Lucy would twist it back at her. The woman was the salt of the earth, but for someone thrice divorced, she was an incorrigible romantic. Which of course might explain why she'd run through so many husbands and delighted in setting up singles. Though as far as Heather knew, poor Lucy had yet to successfully pick a good match.

"Oh, my." Lucy lifted her nose to the sky. "I do believe I forgot to turn the oven off. You'd better take this up to Mr. Harper for me."

Without giving her a chance to accept or back out, Lucy shoved the tray at Heather and spun about, scurrying off.

Her grandmother's knitting needles clacked away. Her expression unresponsive. Her eyes twinkling. Whether the woman was oblivious or playing coy, Heather hadn't a clue. She always wondered how much of what went on did her grandmother really see. Blowing out a resigned sigh, she stood, tray in hand. At least he wasn't working in the shed.

Grams swung the yarn around the needle, pulled it through, pinched her lips and frowned. "I don't think it's supposed to look like this."

Heather didn't think so either, but then again, that could be why the one-time scarf was on its way to baby blankethood.

Setting her work down on her lap, Grams looked up at Heather and smiled. "I forgot to mention."

"What's?" Gripping the handles of the tray more firmly, Heather braced herself for some more matchmaking insight.

"Your sister is upstairs."

"Rose?" Her sister, the museum curator, was almost as bad about coming to the lake as she was. To have both of them here on a Thursday afternoon could be the closest thing to a miracle since that commercial jetliner landed on the Hudson.

Grams returned to winding yarn between clacking needles. "Violet."

Now that made more sense. Where she and Rose were more rigid in their routines, Violet was as flexible as a rubber band. "Which room is she in?"

"Next to you."

"Thanks." Heather kissed her on the cheek and carefully balancing the tray, dashed up the stairs. Normally when she or her sisters came to the lake they'd stay at their mother's cottage. As each of his daughters married, the General had gifted them one of the smaller two bedroom cottages that peppered the Hart land. The disadvantage of having a socialite mother was that once her daughters were grown and gone, there was only so much free time that could be spent on charities and volunteer work. Every so often her mother's abundance of free time meant a change to the cottage. Last week her mother had kept her awake and on the phone for almost an hour filling her in with painful detail of every design choice from imported tile for the backsplash to the flaky Boston artist hired to hand-paint a mural in the living room. If her parents weren't at a conference in Hawaii for her dad, no doubt her mother would be here now bombarding her with paint swatches and hardware samples. The last cottage at the bottom of the hill at the far end of the property, the original six hundred square foot summer home now sported closer to a thousand and by winter a state of the art kitchen would be among its assets.

With Heather's every step the sound of crashing waves intensified. By the time she reached the end of the long hallway and opened the door, a small part of her almost expected to find the rushing Atlantic on the other side. On the floor, smack dab in the center of the room, legs crossed, eyes closed, wrists resting on her knees, and hands palms up, her sister Violet really did look to be in a trance.

Peeking one eye open, Violet spied her sister and sprang to her feet.

Heather set the tray down and pulled her sister into a bear hug. "Am I disturbing your journey to inner peace?"

"Nah," Violet held on a second longer, "I'll find it later."

They spoke on the phone every few days, but not until this very minute did Heather realize how much she missed being face to face with her baby sister. "I thought you weren't coming up until Sunday?"

"Changed my mind." Violet shrugged, turning off the wave sounds.

"Just like that?"

"Well," Violet flopped onto the twin bed, "it might have had something to do with the heat going out at the studio and my having to cancel the rest of the week's classes."

"The way things break in that building, sounds like your landlady could use her own Jake."

"Jake?" Violet's brow dipped into a sharp V.

"Harper. He's very handy. As a matter of fact, he's here now, fixing a broken shower for the General. Lucy wants me to deliver this to him." Heather retrieved the tray and shifted toward the door.

Violet raised her brows, dipped her chin and sprouted an oh-really grin to bookend the one Lucy had flashed downstairs.

"Don't you start with me. Lucy's already singing her repertoire."

"I didn't say a word. *Yet.* But you have to admit, not a bad example of beefcake."

"Beefcake?"

"Have you seen the man without a shirt?"

"Have you?" Why that thought made Heather feel like pissing on his leg and staking her claim she didn't know. She had no claims to make on Jake or anyone else. She had one goal and it had everything to do with following in Michaelson's footsteps as chief of cardiothoracic surgery, and very little to do with the opposite sex.

"We all have." Violet blinked and nodded. "Oh wait. You stopped swimming in the lake long before Jake's growth spurts took off."

"Do you have any idea how many germs lurk in public waterways?" *Or how embarrassing it is to lose a swimsuit top.*

"Heather, this is our lake where we learned to swim and ski and snorkel. Not the canals of Venice."

"Whatever." She waved her sister off, but an unexpected knot twisted in Heather's gut. A longing she'd never felt before. Didn't understand. And it had nothing to do with the handsome guy down the hall. She'd always wanted to be a doctor. For almost as long as she could remember, nothing else seemed to matter. So what if she'd skipped out on the silly antics of summertime? None of the childhood games she'd missed would have made her a better doctor, a better surgeon. Baby Kyle's life was not dependant on Heather having learned to water ski. The knot in her gut slithered its way up her chest, forcing her to ask an even more important question: would she have been any less competent with a scalpel if she'd taken a little more time to play?

"I have to drop this off." She spun away. The need to escape urged her out the door.

"Okay," Violet called after her, "but meet me downstairs. Finding inner peace works up an appetite. And sis?"

"Yeah?" She paused half way to the bathroom.

Violet winked. "Don't do anything I wouldn't do."

Right. Like that would ever happen.

# CHAPTER SIX

"Lucy sent this up."

Jake didn't have to turn around to see who was standing behind him. In the last several hours of the day, Heather's sweet timbre was deeply, and he feared permanently, etched in his memory. "Thank you."

As he took a step forward, Heather took one in retreat and leaned against the doorjamb. He wasn't really thirsty for lemonade, he'd had his fill at Mrs. Norton's, but he couldn't resist the need to turn and drink in a long glimpse of Heather. "Hard to turn down Lucy's lemonade."

"That much I remember." Her lazy smile distorted into a more saddened version.

Everyone remembered Lucy's fresh squeezed lemonade, but it didn't require such a sour expression. "What's up?"

She pushed away from the wall and shook her head. "Just being a little silly. And perhaps a tad self-pitying too."

"What do you mean?" Setting the empty glass down, he couldn't understand what this new attitude was all about. It seemed so unlike the woman who'd mastered her way to the top in what was still most definitely a man's field, nor the woman he'd watched with dogged determination the previous day protect her grandfather, or helped him earlier today to do something nice for a sweet old lady.

"I loved this place as a kid. Summers here are some of the best childhood memories I have."

He nodded. Anyone who grew up at the lake understood that. The lake was a throw back to the days when parents let their kids out at daybreak and didn't expect them home until sunset. And when it came to the Point at Hart House, maybe even later than that. "I detect a but coming."

"I don't know. Talking with Violet just now it seems that apparently my childhood ended before everyone else's."

"I don't understand."

She shrugged. "I never learned to water-ski."

"Excuse me?" That wasn't what he'd expected.

"While everyone was having fun at the lake, water-skiing, paddle boating, or generally cavorting in and around the water as teens, I read, read and read."

He nodded. "I remember. From the porch outside your cabin. You had a birds-eye view of the beach and the Point. I often wondered how you could resist coming out to join the fun."

"I never noticed. I was excited to learn about how the human body worked. To some day make a difference." A sincere smile was back in place. "By the time I took biology in high school, I probably knew more about anatomy than my teacher."

"You do realize you're the only person I know whose face could light up mentioning high school biology?" He took a step back and gave another quick turn to the handles he'd just installed, making sure they didn't fall off again any time soon. Gathering his tools, he turned to catch Heather's perplexed stare. "Don't look so surprised. Is this about missing out on a little summer water sports or something else?"

Heather shrugged. "At the time, whenever one of my sisters or cousins came in from all night on the beach telling ghost stories or dancing with their favorite boy for the summer, or bragging about how many times they made a rock skip—"

"I think your sister Violet still holds the record."

"Yeah, well." She blew out a sigh. "I never bothered to learn half the things they did. I brushed it off. Nowhere on the med school applications does it ask if you can skip stones or water ski. Never mind dance on the beach. For me, playing some stupid game like spin the bottle—"

"Or truth or dare," he interjected.

One side of her mouth tilted up in a weak attempt at a smile. "Or truth or dare, I considered them to be highly overrated. Even the few times I'd get roped into a silly game, I'd walk away thinking what a waste of time."

"And now you don't? Now you wonder if you missed out on more? Is that it?"

"Maybe. Or I'm just overreacting and need to get a grip." She sucked in a long breath, exhaled a deep sigh and forced a broad smile that didn't quite reach her eyes. "Dinner should be about ready and my taste buds are clamoring for anything Lucy cooks."

He wiped his hands on a rag and threw it into his bag. The woman standing in front of him was smart, successful, beautiful, and right now whatever her sister had recently said had struck deep, and he didn't have a clue what to do or say to make it better. Much to his surprise, he really wanted to be the one to put the sparkle back in her eyes. Maybe Tom was right, he needed to get out more.

● ● ● ●

"What in heaven's name do you have there?" Heather came off the bottom step in time to see her sister and cousin struggle their way into the house with a massive box.

Callie dropped her side of the cardboard container. "Varsity girl's basketball game was cancelled. The other team's bus broke down on route. Decided it was fate's way of telling me today would be a great day to go broke saving money at the warehouse store."

"Which one?" Heather hurried to her cousin's side, reaching for a free corner of the oversized carton and wondered if there was a dead body, or two, in the box.

"Does it matter?" Violet shifted sideways to avoid losing her grip.

"Whoa." Coming from the hall, Jake hurried across the massive entry to the women, and placing a hand at each corner, lifted the weight from Violet. "You should have called me."

"You were finishing the bathroom," Callie huffed.

"I'm finished for the day." He glanced over his shoulder. "Where is this going?"

Callie's pace slowed. "Right here is looking really good to me about now."

The box landed on the hardwood floors with a thud.

"What is it?" Heather scanned the box for any hint of its contents.

Callie straightened, brushing her hands together. "New recliner. Leather."

The others in the room eyed the box suspiciously.

"Doesn't seem the right size for a recliner." Violet tilted her head to one side as if that might make a difference.

Callie shrugged. "It will when we put it together."

"We?" Surprise rang out loud and clear in Heather's tone.

"Yeah," Violet choked on a laugh. "What's this *we*, Kemosabe?"

"Let me take a stab at this." Jake smiled at the three women. "Some assembly required?"

Callie tapped the tip of her nose with her finger. "Very good."

"And just who is going to do some of this assembly?" Violet hefted her hands onto her hips. "Because I know you said we, but the only screwdriver I'm handy with involves orange juice."

Heather shook her head back and forth. "Don't look at me. Scalpels don't have anything in common with a screwdriver."

"Well," Violet squeaked, "they are both sharp."

"Which won't do a thing for assembling a recliner." Heather swung her attention from her sister to her cousin. "And if it's yours, why did you bring it here?"

"If two heads are better than one, three should be better than two. Add six hands and putting this thing together should be a piece of cake. It can't weigh anymore to haul it down to my place than the box would have."

"I think I know why they don't ask her to teach math." Violet shook her head at the box. "I don't care how many heads and hands we have, this is a bad idea."

"Ladies." Jake smiled and taking his keys from his pocket, cut the top of the box open. "I'm sure we can handle this."

Violet rolled her eyes. "There's that *we* again."

"Okay." Jake's laughter rumbled low in his chest. "*I* can handle this."

"We can't make you do that." Heather put her hand on his arm. The warmth of his skin under her fingertips had her instantly regretting the move. The way his hands stilled and his gaze latched onto hers, she was sure he felt the heat as well. Oh, she really did need to get out of the hospital more.

"You're not *making* me." He turned back to the box and ripped up the flaps. "I want to."

"Well." Violet spun about. "I don't mean to be rude. You know, open box and run, but before this thing steals what's left of my positive energy, I'm going to return upstairs and work on my inner peace. Someone call me when dinner's ready."

Heather watched her sister exit the room and start up the stairs before turning back to Jake and the box.

Beside her, Callie shook her head at her cousin. "I hate it when she goes all yogi on us."

Reaching into the big box, Heather pulled out a plastic packet with papers, miscellaneous nuts, bolts, washers along with a few more things she didn't have a clue what they were, and waved them at her two cohorts. "I'll play navigator and read the directions."

Jake's affirmative response bore an astounding resemblance to the grunt in a caveman comedy routine. After he'd torn the box apart and spread the contents around him in the open space, he surveyed the items, reached for his tool bag, and pulling out a screwdriver and funny looking pair of pliers—at least Heather thought they were pliers—he began assembling two parts.

"The directions," Heather turned the page to glance at the diagram and then looked back to the instructions, "say to start with that part over there."

Another caveman like grunt accompanied a quick glance by Jake in the direction of her finger before he continued what he was doing.

"I'll be right back with a garbage bag for some of this mess." Callie waved her arm at the scattered strips of cardboard and packing foam.

"Sounds good." Heather didn't want her grandmother or Lucy coming in and seeing the huge mess they were making.

Occasionally pausing to look up or ask for a screw or washer, Jake mostly went to task attaching wooden pieces that promised to transform this jumble of parts into a recliner.

"Are you sure you don't want to look at this?" Heather tried dangling the instructions in his direction.

"Don't need it. Hand me that other screw, please."

Heather looked around a second.

"The long one," Jake explained.

Without letting go of the instructions no one was following,

Heather shifted around Callie, now gathering the bits and pieces of cardboard and packing, and handed Jake the long bolt.

Looking from the bag in her hand, to Jake, to Heather and back, Callie blew out a small sigh. "I think I'm going to get a pop. Anyone want something?"

Jake mumbled *no thanks*, and Heather simply shook her head and looked down at the paper in front of her in an effort to compare it to what Jake was doing.

Studying the diagram, she could feel the growing pressure between her brows. It made absolutely no sense that she could reconstruct tiny vessels in the most powerful muscular organ in the human body—the heart—and for the life of her couldn't tell if what he was doing to the chair was anything close to correct. "How do you know what to do?"

He shrugged. "Just working it out as I go."

"As you go? But I have the instructions." What kind of plan is *as-you-go*? "Maybe you should—"

The sharp glare he tossed in her direction silenced her attempt to get him to look at the paper one more time with more precision and speed than any words could.

"Well, it's starting to look like a chair." Callie walked into the room and smiled.

And it was. A rather nice chair at that.

"There you go." Jake pushed to his feet and took a step back, sporting a satisfied smile. "After closing tomorrow I'll have Tom come help me move it to your place."

"Thanks. I can probably wrangle someone from school to come help."

"Sure. If you run into any trouble, let me know." Jake stretched his arm out at Callie. "These were left over."

Left over? Heather looked down at the list of items that came in the box. "There aren't supposed to be parts left over. Whoever designed this chair meant for all the parts to be used. Not some of them." Heather's sense of rule and order had her wanting to stomp her feet and shout *this is not how it's done*. She couldn't do heart surgery and have 'parts' left over.

"We didn't need them." Jake flopped into the seat and flipped the handle to recline.

Any second Heather expected him to go flying backwards or the entire thing to fall out from under him, proving why he should have followed the directions. He kicked the footrest closed and pulled the handle a few more times and with every movement Heather held her breath.

"You're all set." Jake stood and smiled at Callie.

"I can't thank you enough. I'm sure we'd have figured it out eventually, but I'm not even a little bit nervous about trying it out now." Rubbing her hands together more enthusiastically, Callie collapsed into the chair and flipped back and forth a few times, giggling like a schoolgirl. "This is so cool. I've been wanting a comfy TV chair that would fit in my place for a while, but anything I liked at the furniture stores cost an arm and a leg."

"Glad I could help." Jake picked up his tool bag and took a few steps to stand beside Heather.

"Do you always do things that way?" she asked.

He looked at her, his brow creased in thought. "Do what?"

"Wing it. Not have a plan, ignore instructions, or accept help from others."

His gaze shifted from her, to the chair, and down to the instructions she still held in her hand and he smiled. "Sometimes it's better to just dive in, and this time, I didn't need the help. But I'll keep you in mind for next time."

Flashing her a disarming smile and passing Callie with a departing high five, he left them standing by the chair. With a final wave, he called over his shoulder, "I'll be back tomorrow to patch the hole I made in the wall."

She glanced down at the instructions then up at the ceiling. *Parts left over*. How did anyone live like that?

# CHAPTER SEVEN

Sunlight poured into the dining room of the lake house. At one end of the table, Heather's grandmother sat, only a tea cup within reach, her hands already busy working on the current and somewhat lopsided knitting endeavor. Across the table, her grandfather held the morning paper in one hand while scratching the top of Lady's head with the other. Sarge lay sprawled on the floor at his other side, his gaze tracking his humans.

A small sense of relief licked at Heather's insides, not enough to put her totally at ease, but relief nonetheless. Until yesterday, her career military grandfather had never slept in a day in his life. The times he would be home with everyone at the lake, he ran the house much like he would a military base. His children and grandchildren had to be up and dressed for breakfast bright and early. Sometimes too early.

Grams had to work extra hard to keep him from imposing similar rules on guests. Which was why it had been a bit of a shock yesterday morning to find him still in bed when she'd come down for breakfast. Though she'd barely heard him cough since arriving, being tired was another symptom of anything as simple as a touch of anemia to a sign of heart disease.

"Good morning." Her sister floated into the room. Violet had always had a natural sense of grace. Had she not become a yoga instructor, she probably could have become one helluva ballerina.

Violet loaded her dish with Lucy's special breakfast casserole, toast, bacon, a glob of cream cheese, and a scoop of hash browns.

Looking up from her knitting as Violet slid into the seat beside her, Grams' gaze dropped to the mountain of food on Violet's plate. "Anyone would think you haven't had a decent meal in weeks."

"I haven't." Violet spread her napkin across her lap. "I've been on a juice cleanse."

Grams rolled her eyes. "In my day, we didn't worry about toxins, cleansing or any of that nonsense."

"That's because in your day the food supply wasn't being poisoned with genetic mutations, pesticides, and enough sugar to rot a rhino's horn."

"Don't be silly, dear." Her grandmother returned her attention to the yarn in her lap. "Rhinos don't eat with their horns."

Heather smiled at her grandmother's cavalier response to Violet's mini tirade on the state of society. Having taken only a small serving of the casserole and poured herself a glass of juice, Heather took the seat on her sister's other side.

The General folded his paper and set it down beside him. "It's a wonderful sight, both you girls in the same room. All we need is for your sister Rose to join us on Sunday and I dare say it may be the first time in years we'll have had all three Preston girls at the lake at the same time."

"Don't hold your breath waiting for Rose." Violet waved a fork at her grandfather. "The museum has a new exhibit opening next month. The way she talks, it's the biggest thing to hit Boston since King Tut. From the sound of it, this is the most responsibility her boss has ever entrusted her with and I don't think she's getting much sleep, never mind taking time to come to the lake."

"Really?" Heather stabbed at her food. "She hasn't said a word to me about it. What's the exhibit?"

"Something about the art of the masters from Versailles." Violet shrugged. "I asked one little question and she clammed up on me."

"What was the question?" the General asked.

"Would the museum let the patrons eat cake?" Violet hefted one shoulder in a what's-a-girl-to-do shrug. "She must not be a fan of Marie Antoinette."

Heather smothered a laughed. "Yeah. I can see where that would not have gone over very well with Rose." Her sister had many wonderful qualities; a sense of humor when it came to her work was rarely one of them.

"Well." Grams wrapped her knitting up, stuffed it in the bag, and circled around to her husband. "I'm going to freshen up and then I'll be ready to go to Nora's."

The General snatched her hand in his, squeezed, and with eyes riveted on her, nodded. "I'll get the car."

"Nora's?" Heather asked.

"Yes, dear. She owns the new yarn shop at the Olla Podrida."

"The what?" Had Heather really been gone so long that she didn't have even a clue who or what her grandmother was talking about?

Her grandfather blew out a short sigh. "Some developer from out west bought the old shopping village and gave it that ridiculous name."

"It's not ridiculous, dear." Grams patted her husband's shoulder. "It sounds very artsy."

"It means rotten pot," he groused. "Who in their right mind takes a smattering of old shops, spends a small fortune to turn it into a cohesive arts and crafts Mecca of the northeast and then names it the Rotten Pot?"

"He does have a point, Grams." Violet shoved the last forkful of food into her mouth.

"Well," Heather started. If she were going to get her grandfather into the doctor's office, he couldn't be driving her grandmother back and forth across the lake. "I'm sure Violet would love to give you a ride."

"I would?" Violet looked to her sister.

Heather gave her younger sibling a kick under the table and holding her hands low out of her grandmother's line of sight, jerked her thumb at her grandfather.

"That's right." Violet suddenly aware, smiled up at her grandmother. "I would."

"And then the General and I can have some quality time together." Heather cast a stern eye at her grandfather. "In town."

"Oh." Grams slid her hand from her husband's shoulder. "Well, of course. I see your grandfather all the time."

"Nonsense." The General gave Lady one last pat and stood. "I'll drive you."

"General." Heather did her best to use the same stern voice she'd use with a young intern.

The General hooked his hand at his wife's elbow. "I'll have plenty of time to visit with Heather after we return from the Rotten

Pot." Without so much as a glance in her direction, her grandfather escorted his wife and two dogs out of the dining room.

"Oh, he is going to be a pill about this, isn't he?" Violet kept her gaze on the now empty doorway.

Heather sucked in a long deep breath and quickly blew it out. "What are we going to do with him?"

"Is it really that bad?" Worry gleamed in Violet's eyes the same as it had with the cousins the other night.

"I honestly don't know. But it's the General and I don't want this to be the time we blow something off as ordinary and it turns out to be anything but."

"He does look awfully healthy to me," Violet said meekly.

"Yeah," Heather agreed. "And I'd like to keep him that way." *No matter what it takes.*

•  •  •  •

"Top of the morning to you, Fiona Maureen." The hint of an Irish accent carried from behind the counter across the length of the small general store.

Fiona Hart smiled at the only person in town who called her by her full Christian name. One picked by her very Irish grandmother. The same woman who'd taught Fiona the proper response to the traditional greeting. "And the rest of the day to you, Mary Kathleen."

Mary Kathleen O'Leary, Katie to most of the town, exemplified walking sunshine. The woman always had a smile, often had a story, never had a complaint, and every Irishman within one hundred miles knew to come shopping at the One Stop if they were feeling a longing for all things shamrock or blarney. Born and raised in this very town at the knee of her immigrant grandmother, Katie teased most of her life that some people were multi-lingual, but she on the other hand was semi-lingual. Her grandmom's heavy Irish accent had been the foundation of her verbal skills for so long that despite years in school and all the life that followed, she never quite lost the Irish lilt in her English.

As far as Fiona Lawford Hart was concerned, that was a good thing. Katie and her family reminded Fiona of her favorite grandmother and that always made her feel young at heart. "Lucy has given up on baking a decent soda bread."

Katie's smile stretched across her face. "Indeed, there is a trick to it."

"One you'd not be sharing."

Shaking her head, Katie continued to smile. "Promised my sainted grandmother that her secret would only be shared with an O'Leary, and only the ones with a gift in the kitchen. My poor mum couldn't boil a decent corned beef if her life depended on it. Will that be one loaf or two?"

"Better make it four. We have a rather busy house this week."

"Oh." Katie's brows rose high on her forehead. "And who might that be?"

"Violet and Heather. Hoping they might entice Iris and Zinnia to drive up from NY. "

"Ah, now that would be grand."

"Yes," Fiona smiled. "It would." She and the General did so enjoy having the girls around, though she wouldn't mind having a few little ones around again. So many of her friends were having great grandbaby after grandbaby and Fiona had yet to gain even one grandson-in-law.

"Need some help?" The General came up to his wife's side.

"I thought you were going to wait for me in the car?"

"It got lonesome." His voice came out only slightly above a whisper but by the cute way Katie's lips curled up in the corners, he'd obviously said so loud enough for her to hear.

Fiona's heart warmed at the soft spoken words. For all the years she'd raised her family alone. For all the deployments that bled into the next. For all the towns they'd passed through with hardly enough time to make a home. For all the fears kept hidden behind a brave façade, those few words and the love in his eyes, the love that had always been in his eyes, made every last minute worthwhile.

And this was what she prayed for daily for all her darling granddaughters.

• • • •

How Heather got roped into planting bulbs in the front garden, she had no idea. One minute she was standing in the dining room after lunch, hands on her hips, `wondering how much longer her grandparents would be gone and the next thing Lucy had her outside with miscellaneous bags of fresh bulbs, a hand trowel, gardening soil, and parting words of *not too close together* followed a moment later by *and not upside down.*

Holding the first bulb about the size of a nickel in her hand, she debated exactly which end was right side up. She'd watched Lucy and her Grandmother plant flower bulbs more than once in her life, but even if she had paid attention, there was no way she'd remember all these years later.

Reading the back of the first bag, she scanned the instructions for planting. "When all else fails..." She pulled her phone from her pocket and Googled the flower name on the bag. A few strokes later and she'd determined the narrowed tip was actually down not up. Good thing she hadn't guessed.

One bag held the smaller bulbs and the other the larger ones. The former needed to have a hole dug only five inches deep while the bigger ones needed to be buried eight inches down. She glanced around the array of tools and supplies Lucy had left with her. Nowhere was there a ruler.

Trowel in hand, she began digging holes in clusters. The plan was simple. Dig down as far as her fist and then get a ruler from inside to determine how much more dirt to remove to reach the five and eight inch lengths.

"You've been busy," a smooth deep voice sounded behind her.

No need to look up, she knew by the goose bumps spreading up her arm who the voice belonged to. Ready to move to the other side, she pushed to her feet. "Helping Lucy while I wait for my grandfather to return." Looking down at her handy work, the one side of the garden now peppered with haphazard holes resembled the work of a drunken gopher. If the idea was supposed to be no rhyme or reason to the bed, she'd clearly succeeded. Having used her cell phone to measure the distance between holes hadn't worked out as well as she'd hoped.

"Looks good."

She glanced down again, not sure how he could tell.

"I'm going to patch the sheetrock in the bedroom, the one I had to cut out to fix the shower." He waved his arm at the house. "Need anything from inside before I get started?"

"I was just about to go in and get a ruler." She brushed her hands clean.

"A ruler?"

"To measure."

"That's what a ruler is usually for," he smiled. "But why do you need one?"

What did he mean why? "To know when I've reached the right depth."

His gaze shifted from her dirty hands, to the holes in the ground to the still unturned bed on the other side of the path. "I don't think it's supposed to be an exact science."

A glass in hand, Lucy hurried down the porch steps. "Thought you might like some fresh limeade. Good for the liver."

It would be except for all the sugar. "Thank you. I was just coming in for a ruler."

A smile pulling at her lips, Lucy looked at the holes and shook her head. "No need, I'll be right back with it." She turned to Jake. "I'll get you a glass too."

"No thanks," he held up his tool bag, "on my way to work."

"Suit yourself." Lucy shrugged, then sporting a wide grin, softly sang "It Only Takes a Moment," from Hello Dolly all the way up the porch steps.

Brushing some dirt from her lap, Heather hoped the woman wasn't up to something Heather would live to regret.

"Would you like some help?" Jake set his tool bag on the ground.

Heather shook her head. "I think I can handle planting a few flower bulbs." At least *she* knew how to follow instructions. Though she would have preferred it if Lucy had given her a plan for the layout.

"Here you go." Looking just a tad too happy, Lucy bounced down the steps waving a ruler at her.

"Thanks." Heather stood a moment watching the woman hurry

back up the stairs, still singing, before kneeling on the foam pad. Holding the ruler center of the hole with one hand, she dug at the dirt with the trowel in the other.

Jake squatted beside her. "I don't think Lucy, or your grandmother, use a ruler."

"Don't you have a wall to fix?" Heather leaned back on her heels.

Rolling his eyes skyward, Jake shoved upright, grabbed his bag and walked up the wooden steps. The screen door squeaked open and from the short distance, Jake's voice carried easily, "You know, sometimes it's all right to eyeball it."

# CHAPTER EIGHT

Taking a step back to survey the work, Jake wiped his hands on a nearby rag. No one would know there'd ever been a hole cut into the adjoining wall. He glanced around the bedroom. Filled with an eclectic combination of modern pieces blended with antiques that had no doubt been in the family for generations, the room looked like it had fallen out of any country magazine. Charm, comfort and love radiated from every corner.

Tomorrow he'd be back to paint and the job would be all finished—and he'd be out of excuses to see Heather. Not that it mattered, a few more days and she'd be on her way back to Boston.

"Oh, that does look good." The object of his musings stepped into the room.

"How'd the flowers turn out?"

"Fine." She shifted her weight and shrugged before taking a step forward. "It was really nice of you to make time to do this for my grandfather."

"That's what neighbors are for, to help when they can."

She studied him just long enough to have an edge of discomfort begin to creep up his spine. He hoped she wasn't building up steam for a tongue lashing because of his earlier comment from the porch door about eyeballing a situation over being so rigidly precise.

A smile teetered at one side of her mouth. "You do that a lot, don't you. Like with Mrs. Norton."

He shrugged, tossing the rag aside. The extra attention definitely made him uncomfortable. "Not much. Once in awhile."

"Well, the last few days you've had more than your share of being neighborly."

Gathering up the tarp and other tools, Jake knew she was studying him again. It made him feel a bit like a rat in a maze. Or a bug under a microscope. "So," he picked up his bag, "did you learn anything more about the General's health?"

"No." Her shoulders slumped and her lips pressed tightly together before she straightened again and forced a smile. "But we have a plan."

"A plan?"

"Yes. Since neither the General nor his doctor are cooperating, I talked with Lucy, Violet and my cousins and everyone who's in Lawford, even Lily and Cindy, are coming for dinner. Lucy's making his favorite corned beef and cabbage with Rosemary roasted potato instead of boiled, and Lily's baking his favorite kolackys. After he's been well fed and buttered up with dessert, I'm going to give him a little medical exam."

"And the cousins are here for... reinforcements?"

Her shoulders slipped again. "Yeah. I just hope the sheer number of us is enough and we don't have to call in the SEALs to tie him down and allow me take a few vitals and listen to his chest."

"I'm not sure the entire Marine Corps could accomplish that. Few servicemen like to butt horns with a general."

"True."

"Hey, you two." Violet popped her head into the doorway. "Poppy and Callie are downstairs. Lucy says we have five minutes to try a kolacky before she puts them away so we don't spoil dinner."

"Seriously?" Heather put her hands on her hips. "I think we'll always be five years old in her mind."

"Don't complain," Violet spun around. "If it involves homemade cookies or kolackys I can refrain from growing up."

At the kitchen island, both Callie and Poppy sat, already nibbling on one of Lily's kolacky's

The family cook shoved a dish at Jake. "Saved you two."

"No fair." Callie's gaze followed the plate sliding across the counter. "Why does he get two?"

For the big bad gym teacher, Callie was whining like, well, a girl—of the teenage variety. Jake had to swallow his laughter. Not that he'd heard that many teenagers whining of late, but the memory of his high school girlfriend constantly fussing about one little thing or another popped into his head large as life.

"Because," Lucy pointed a thumb in Jake's direction, "that man worked hard today. And yesterday. And the day before that."

"I dealt with ninth, tenth and eleventh graders all day, and yesterday, and the day before, not to mention a team of estrogen-charged basketball players on edge about the upcoming semi finals." Callie glared. "I deserve the whole batch."

This time Jake did laugh out loud. "She does have a point."

Lucy harrumphed and turned away. "Corned beef will be served in ten minutes."

Heather's grandmother practically floated into the room. Dressed in a bright floor length muumuu of some kind that offset her silver white chin length hair and bright blue eyes, the lady would fit in with any classic Hollywood movie star from the glamour days. In contrast, she could still easily blend in with the artists across the lake. Eyes sparkling at the dish of fresh baked goods the housekeeper held in her hands, Mrs. Hart's smile widened. "Oh, how wonderful. I keep losing stitches on my new project and I need to take my disappointment out on something sinfully delicious."

"These," Callie pointed to the half-eaten kolacky in her hand, "definitely fit the bill."

"And there's more for dessert," Lily pulled a hot tray from the oven.

The girls' grandmother offered each one in her path a peck on the cheek. "Is your mother on the way?"

"She couldn't make it," Callie muttered through a full mouth. "Wake tonight."

"Really." The silver haired beauty dropped two kolackys on her small plate. "I hadn't heard anyone passed."

The Hart's middle daughter, Virginia, had married the town mortician and inherited the business after his death. Going from stay-at-home mom to single parent and funeral parlor director had been a challenge at first, but Virginia had pulled it off. Most of the time.

"Somebody better be setting the table," Lucy called from the sink.

Several able bodies jumped to their feet, and even though none of the young women lived with their grandmother, the cousins moved about the kitchen gathering utensils, plates, glasses and napkins as though it were a nightly ritual. No one bumped into the other. Everyone remembered exactly which cupboard or drawer held what they were looking for. A twinge of jealousy pinched at Jake. Not only was he an only child, but so were both his parents. The only family he had left were the grandparents in Virginia.

A cold moist nose nudged at his palm then gave one long lick to the back of his hand.

"Well hello there." Jake scratched behind the golden's ear. "Which one are you?"

Mrs. Hart looked up for a second and announced, "That's Lady."

Jake cast his glance from Lady, short for Lady Liberty, to Sarge the identical animal laying in the kitchen doorway. He had no clue how the General's wife could tell them apart at a glance, but just to be sure he dipped his head to peek at her underbelly. Yep. Lady, impatient with the pause in his attention, pressed her nose under his fingers and shoved his hand up and onto her head. The forceful motion was clearly dog-speak for keep scratching.

"What's she doing in here?" Pausing to look down at the dog, Heather carried a stack of dishes to the dining room.

Poppy came behind her laden with soda bread and salad. "Wonder why they left the General's side."

"Is he okay?" Callie turned and popping her head into the hall, scanned the area for her grandfather.

"I'm sure he's fine." Mrs. Hart stood from the kitchen table. "The General is probably taking an afternoon nap and the dogs are too smart to give up a chance for the lot of you to love on them."

"Nap?" On her way back to the kitchen, Heather stopped, frowning at her grandmother. "Since when does the General take a nap this time of day?"

"Heather, dear," her grandmother patted Heather's arm on her way out the door, "there's a lot to be said for a nice afternoon snooze."

On his feet and at her side, Sarge rubbed against Heather, almost as if saying listen to your grandmother, before turning and following his master's wife to the dining room. Abandoning Jake, Lady pranced after her cohort.

"I know that look." Poppy eased beside her cousin. "What are you thinking?"

She looked at Jake as though expecting him to tell her what to say, gave him an almost imperceptible shake of her head, and offered a plastic smile. "Grams is right. Some days I'd kill for an afternoon nap."

"And you're perfectly healthy," Lucy said. "Supper's ready. Everyone in the dining room, and Jake—"

"Yes, ma'am?"

"Be a sweetheart and knock on the General's door to let him know it's chow time."

Bobbing his head, he turned to go up the massive staircase when Fiona Hart leaned into the hall. "We've saved a seat for you, Jake." And then she disappeared into the dining room without waiting for a response. Not that he had any intention of doing anything other than enjoying a few more hours of Dr. Heather Preston's company.

● ● ● ●

"That was delicious as usual, Lucy." Violet carried two dishes into the kitchen. Heaven forbid anyone stack the plates for faster cleanup. Lucy would have had a nest of canaries.

"Best meal I've had in ages." Heather reached over and picked up Jake's plate along with her own. He in turn took their drinking glasses in hand to follow when the General pulled him aside.

Normally when Heather made it to the lake house for a family dinner, she and her sisters would sit on the side of the table closest to the window. This evening, every time she tried to weave around to the other side of the dining room, either Lady or Sarge meandered in front of her, or merely plopped at her feet, tail wagging like a battery operated broom, and blocking her path. It was almost as though they'd had a conspiracy to keep her from eating supper. By the time the General called the two pups to his side at the head of the table, the only open seat left was on the opposite side between the General and Jake, the two seats to one side of the General usually filled by her New York cousins, Iris and Zinnia.

"Did you hear about Wade Abbot?" In the kitchen, Lucy filled the sink with sudsy water. "He and his wife are having baby number two."

"Uh oh," Poppy muttered softly, her steps slowing. She'd dated

Wade eons ago.

"Want to hide behind me?" Heather hefted a shoulder as if she could block Poppy from Lucy's view.

"Yes, sirree," Lucy continued. "That makes two babies in little more than two years."

Coming through the doorway, Callie froze, plates in hand, and leaned into her sister. "Who's pregnant now?"

Rolling her eyes skyward, Poppy blew out a low huff of exasperated breath. "Wade's wife."

"Whew." Smiling again, Callie muttered, "Thought it was one of my exes."

"He was never mine," Poppy bit back louder than she probably meant to.

"Should have been though." Lucy slid the dirty plates into the sink. "You two made such a lovely couple back then. I told Wade's mama he was perfect for you. Thought for sure that was a match made in heaven."

"We dated one summer." Poppy advanced setting her dishes on the counter. "Not even the whole summer. And I was only fifteen. There was no heaven and no match."

"You tell her," Violet whispered, careful not to let Lucy hear, grabbing an apron from the nearby hook.

Callie touched Heather's arm. "What are the odds we'll make it through coffee without Lucy finding out Steve Carmichael just got engaged?"

At least Heather didn't have to worry. The good thing about not having dated much as a teen, or an undergrad, was there weren't any old boyfriends getting married or raising children for Lucy to trudge up and parade around in conversation like a surrender flag.

"Think Poppy can take the heat if I just sneak out," Callie leaned into her.

Heather whispered to Callie through the side of her mouth, "Chicken."

"Slave driver," Callie quipped quietly.

Heather bit back a laugh. It wouldn't matter to Lucy that Callie's ex, Steve, was on engagement number three and wife number two. All that impacted Lucy's matchmaking streak was that Steve and Callie had dated their last two years of high school, which of course meant if Callie hadn't thrown him over for that college boy, Steve wouldn't be on wife number two. Regardless of the circumstances, Lucy knew just how to needle the girls about their love lives, or lack of.

"You'd think by now," Lucy looked over her shoulder at Poppy, "you'd have met some nice handsome God-fearing man at that church of yours."

"I keep the books." Poppy blew out another small sigh. "I don't run Christian Mingle."

"What about the new organist. He seems nice." Lucy paused and squinting one eye, studied Poppy. "Yes, very nice."

"Now, Lucy." Grams walked straight to the old percolator. The General liked one cup after dinner. Fresh brewed. The old-fashioned way. "Leave the girls alone. They'll find the right men when the time is right. My girls did, so will they." She leaned against Poppy and her lips sweetly brushing against her granddaughter's cheek, Grams whispered, "You'd better get going before she remembers Missy Abbot is having twins this time."

Poppy's face lit up and she threw her arms around the smiling older lady. Casting a quick glance at Heather and back, she eased away from her grandmother. "Thanks, Grams, but I'm going to stick around for a little while longer."

"Yes, indeed. I do appreciate you stepping in for George like this." The General entered the spacious kitchen with Jake at his side. "Lucy, I don't know how tonight's corned beef can be better than the last, but it was. Excellent meal."

"Yes, Lucy." Jake nodded his agreement.

"Coffee will be ready in a few. Why don't you boys go wait on the porch." Grams turned from the counter to face her husband. Violet stifled a smile but Heather let hers show. She'd forgotten how cute it was when her grandmother would refer to her military-tough husband as one of the boys.

The General sidled up beside his wife. Drank her in with his eyes. Gave her a pat on her rump so slight that Heather almost didn't see it before he stepped back. "Capital idea, Fiona."

All these decades of marriage and her grandparents still treated each other like young lovers. The General adored his wife, and whenever Uncle Sam allowed him time at the lake, he'd never missed a chance, big or small, to show his wife just how much he loved her. How many modern men could live up to those expectations? No surprise none of the grandchildren had gotten married yet.

"Anything I can do to help?" Jake asked.

Before her grandmother or Lucy could respond, her grandfather spun to face him, nudging him out of the kitchen. "As a matter of fact, there is. One of the guests in the maple cottage took a paddle boat out on the lake and I could see it knocking against the pier before dinner but didn't have time to better secure it. Would you mind saving these tired old eyes the challenge of dealing with the boat in the dark and make sure it's tied the way it should be?"

"Of course." Jake didn't hesitate to follow the General down the hall.

The percolator began hissing and gurgling and making all sorts of sounds as it prepared to pour out liquid heaven. Maybe if Heather bought a real percolator for the doctor's lounge at the hospital she wouldn't have to drink sludge ever again. *Right*. And maybe she'd find Nessy in their lake tonight.

Heather reached for the extra apron to help with clean up. Nowhere else did she put on an apron to clean up dishes or wipe counters, but it was a required ritual here at the lake house. She always felt like a star on one of those reality cooking shows when she wore one of her grandmother's big old aprons.

"Luce," Lily put a pitcher of tea into the fridge, "do you want me to start drying those pots or serve dessert?"

"Actually," her grandmother pulled out a few cups from the cabinets, "one of you had better go help Jake. Those old boats can get away from a person, even a strong one, pretty easily."

"I'll go." Violet stepped away from her position by the sink and reached behind her back.

"You're already on dish duty." Lucy's hand slid across the sink and lightly brushed Violet's arm. "Let your sister go. She can use some real fresh air."

Though she wasn't exactly overjoyed over the jab about lack of fresh air where she lived, Heather certainly didn't mind the idea of being nominated as official boat assistant to one Mr. Jake Harper. The prospect made her feel way more school-girl giddy than a grown doctor should.

# CHAPTER NINE

"Need a hand?" Heather's voice carried across the Point.

Leaning over the stone edge, Jake sat up. "Not so far." The boat was almost properly secured, but he had a hard time returning his attention to the task at hand. Only a half moon shone and yet the light beamed down on Heather like a spotlight on a runway as she moved closer. Dang was she beautiful.

"You got it?" She kneeled beside him, looking down at the boat rocking gently in the water.

Forcing himself to tear his gaze away and deal with the boat shouldn't have been so difficult.

"Jake?" Confusion laced his name.

"Sorry." He shifted his weight and leaned over. "Almost finished." The guests had done a fine job of tying up the front of the boat but had failed to notice the rope in the rear. Another swirl and quick knot and all was secure. "Done."

"Bravo." She clapped and leaned back, landing on her backside, and laughed. "Oops."

Joining her laughing, he sat beside her. His knees drawn up, he draped his arms casually across them. The moonlight skipping along the lake cast shadows along the shore that bounced against them and had his mind wandering to how lovely she'd look with the water sluicing around her.

"I can't believe how warm it's been for this time of year."

"I know."

She tipped her head up to the stars. "This always was the most peaceful place on earth."

The Harts had one of the best spots on the lake as far as he was concerned. "A month ago and we could have jumped in and gone swimming."

"Are you nuts?" Her head snapped around. "It's not that warm. A month ago and that water would already have been an invitation to hypothermia. It may be nice and sunny in the afternoon, but don't let that fool you. This time of year, the lake has to be frigid."

"Nah, we've swam in it late in the year before." He leaned back on his elbows and suppressed the grin that threatened at the cute way she shook her head at him.

One of the cabins across the creek opened a window and familiar tunes drifted their way. He remembered the song from high school. That time of his life when the kids spent all summer on the Point, and Heather watched youthful antics from a distance. Remembering her words the other night about all the teenage escapades she'd missed out on, he turned to face her. "Did you ever get to dance with a favorite boy on the beach?"

Her face still tilted up to the sky, she merely shook her head.

From the way she'd run off the list last night, he'd figured as much. Pushing to stand, he bowed at the waist and extended his arm. "May I have the honor of this dance?"

Big round eyes blinked up at him. Anyone would have thought he'd asked her to go skinny dipping. Blinking a few more times, she shifted her gaze to the nearest cabins on one side and then to the lake on the left.

"I promise I won't let you fall in." He tried not to fidget waiting for her response.

The hint of a smile teased at one side of her mouth. "I know that. It's just…"

"Just what?"

"Well." She looked across the creek to the source of the music. "I'm not really a very good dancer."

For a moment he wondered if she'd ever been dancing at all. Had she ever put the books down long enough to enjoy herself in high school? "If I promise not to step on your feet will you give it a shot?"

Eyes filled with a plethora of emotions studied him, until finally she accepted his hand and slowly stretched to her full height. "I may regret this."

He certainly hoped not. Twirling her easily against him, he skipped circling his arms around her the way he would have done at a high school dance and opted for the traditional one hand at the small of her back and the other holding her hand in the air beside him. He swayed slowly to one side and back, relieved when the stiffness in her spine relaxed a bit. "See? You're a natural."

That made her head tip back with laughter. "Liar, liar, pants on fire."

Pulling her just a hint closer, he spun them around and when she stayed in step with him, he grinned down at her. "I think maybe you're the one whose pants are smoking."

Her one brow shot up in surprise.

Too late he realized there could have been a better way to say that. "You dance beautifully."

"Thank you." There was just enough moonlight above for him to see her cheeks pinken slightly and the pleased twinkle in her eyes.

The music stopped as suddenly as it had started and he found himself desperately wanting more time. Neither one moved. Not to sway, not to dance, not to separate. Like a magnet drawn to true north they remained joined, unable to pull apart. His pulse hummed to its own tune and nothing could stop him from what he wanted to do next.

● ● ● ●

"Woof."

Lifting his gaze from his laptop and still steaming cup of coffee, retired General Harold Hart took note of Lady at the edge of the porch. Sarge dutifully sat beside him, strategically situated so his hand would be at just the right height to scratch behind the dog's ear if the urge struck. The sound of Sarge's other half had the loveable golden on alert.

"Woof," Lady barked again, her head turning from the distance to where he sat and then back. If the tail weren't wagging rapidly, Harold would have been concerned something or someone unwelcome had breached the perimeter. Not that they had a fence enclosing the family land, but still, the dogs knew better than he did where his land ended and the neighbor's started. When Sarge trotted away to join Lady at the railing, it was almost enough to make Harold pause his messaging on social media and get up to see if it was a squirrel or raccoon that had the attention of both animals, but the conversation was just getting interesting and he had no intention of giving it up for a night crawling critter.

"Woof," Sarge sounded and turned his head from Lady to master. Apparently both dogs were bound and determined to have him come see whatever was lurking around for himself.

"Okay." Harold posted TTYL, logged off, and stood, reminding himself dogs were man's best friend, even at the climactic moment of a military thriller.

Almost smiling, Sarge panted and set his tail to wagging faster than Lady's.

"All right. What critter has your.... Well, well." If not for the moonlight it might have taken him longer to notice the silhouettes in the distance—dancing. "How about that?"

Lady woofed and moved around so the retired general was flanked by a dog on either side. Together the three watched the couple gently swaying in the distance. Harold smiled. Wouldn't this make for interesting conversation next time he chatted with Gene.

Harold's firstborn grandbaby was one helluva surgeon and he couldn't have been prouder of her if she'd single handedly cured all heart disease, but even boots on the ground soldiers got some R&R. Setting a hand atop either dogs' head, he gently patted them. "Glad someone around here still has sharp eyes."

Before settling back into his favorite chair, he glanced from the dogs still staring intently at the shore, tails wagging double time, to the shadowed figures in the distance.

"Stall tactics?" His loving bride of decades came to stand beside him.

The woman always could read him like a book. "Just admiring the view."

"You know you can't put her off forever."

Of course he could. He hadn't made General in the Marine Corps by being soft.

"And if she corners Doc Wilkins..." her words hung.

That might be more of a problem. Unless he could drop chaff. Sometimes all a person needed to distract a dog after steak was a good bone.

His Fiona linked her arm with his. "They do make a nice couple."

"That they do," he agreed, "that they do."

• • • •

How long had it been since Heather had been kissed? She had no idea right now. As a matter of fact, the way Jake's lips gently pressed against hers, she wasn't sure she had really ever been kissed. Once again music streamed from the open window across the creek. This time she recognized the tune as Al Green's, "Let's Stay Together." Her heart beat in rhythm to the soulful tune, and right about now, she wanted to do exactly as the lyrics encouraged, good or bad, happy or sad, she could stay together this way for pretty darn near forever. His head tilted slightly at the same second his arms pulled her closer and all thought slid away. In a warm haze she leaned into him. The one thing she was sure of, she had most definitely never been kissed like this before.

The murmur of voices in the distance grew closer. Annoyingly closer. The sound finally loud enough for Jake to sigh against her lips and slowly ease back. "I, uh," he took a step in retreat, "probably should not have done that."

Still heady from the thrum of sensations due to a single mind-blowing kiss, it took an extra beat to process his words.

His gaze, etched with concern, studied hers. She could almost see the stream of thoughts rushing around in his head. One in particular must have won out, because the corners of his mouth tipped up in a hesitant smile. "Since you haven't hauled off and hit me, I'm going to admit, I'm dang glad I did."

Violet's voice rang out, "Ooh, are we going to have another bonfire?"

Surprised to see Violet approaching by herself, Heather looked around for the other voice. It took a second to realize Vi held her phone in the palm of her hand face-up. *Speakerphone.* Though she supposed that was better than having had Violet walk up in silence and catch them in a very public display of affection. Affection? She took another step back. Affection? "No," she muttered, "not a bonfire." At least not the traditional kind. "Just tying up the boat. We still need to deal with the General."

"That's right. Too bad." Violet slid the phone into a back pocket. "That was Rose. I'm not sure things are going so well with this new exhibit."

"She said that?" Heather took a step in her sister's direction, her concern for her other sibling shaking her mind clear of how her lips still tingled. She focused on Violet's approach.

Rose was the perfect combination of Violet and herself. The woman never met a stranger. She could schmooze with the Queen of England and not bat an eye. Five minutes with her sister Rose and Ebenezer Scrooge would be donating his entire art collection. Hardworking, diligent, detail oriented, and amazingly efficient, she was equally comfortable relaxing on the deck chair with a good book as she was in a business suit with a tight deadline. She rarely asked for help and Heather couldn't remember the last time she'd heard her sister complain. About anything.

Violet shrugged. "Not in those exact words but I could feel the negative vibes coming off and read between the lines."

Reading between the lines gave Heather reason to frown and contemplate the situation. As much as the family made fun of Violet for her white noise, contemplative tendencies, and excessive concerns with mother nature, the woman's gut instincts when it came to reading people and situations—or auras as she called them—were sometimes surprisingly good. On the other hand, Rose's ability to handle difficult bosses, difficult situations, and difficult clients left Heather wondering if Violet was reading too much into whatever their sister had said. She certainly hoped it was the latter.

"Well." Jake sucked in a long breath and pivoted around. "I'd better get going. Having me around might give the General an excuse to get out of an exam."

Heather wanted to shout no, stop, wait, lets talk, but the practical common sense side of her that had always given a situation its due diligence snatched the words from her mouth and she merely nodded.

"Sure you don't want to stick around for a bonfire after the big showdown? I bet I could rustle up a bottle of wine."

Jake shook his head. "Wouldn't want to overstay my welcome."

"Nonsense," Violet answered quickly. For a woman who was so proud of her aura reading skills, she was failing miserably at sensing the awkwardness that sprang up between Jake and Heather like a sudden squall over a tempestuous sea.

"I really do need to go." He cast a glance in Heather's direction and shoving his hands in his pocket, kicked at a large pebble. "See you tomorrow?"

"Yes," she blurted before her practical side could filter her enthusiasm.

A sweet smile took over his face and her lips tingled once again. What was she getting herself into?

"Yoo-hoo." Violet waved her hand in her sister's face.

Blinking, Heather dragged her gaze away from Jake's departing back and turned to her sister. "Sorry, my mind wandered."

Violet stared toward the circular drive where Jake was climbing into his car and smiled. "Yeah, I can see where a girl wouldn't mind doing a little wandering around that particular piece of real estate."

"Violet," Heather scolded, though she had no idea why since her sister had only said the truth.

"Don't get all nose out of joint around me. I know there's a red-blooded female hiding somewhere under that all-business doctor's white coat of yours and if Jake's the one to uncover her you won't hear any objection from me. He's one of the genuine nice guys."

"He is, isn't he?" Her gaze drifted back to the house and the now empty driveway.

"Uh oh."

Heather spun around to fully face her sister. "Uh oh, what?"

"I've seen that look before."

"What look?"

"The one you had after a tour of Stanford. After looking at about half a dozen med schools closer to home, you spent one lousy day at Stanford and decided that was where you wanted to go."

"What the hell are you talking about?" Shaking her head, Heather turned on her heel and started up the path to the house. She had a medical exam to perform on one stubborn retired general.

Violet followed on her heels, laughing. "Oh, this is going to be fun."

"I repeat," Heather paused looking over her shoulder, "what are you talking about?"

"Being the oldest, for a long while we all thought you would be the first to fall in love, but being the one who hasn't had a personal life in… well, forever, I didn't *expect* you to be the first to fall."

Shaking her head again, Heather continued on track to the house. Her sister had totally lost her mind. She was turning into the old busy bodies in town. The merry widows known for playing matchmaker with all the singles since the dawn of time. "Have you been nipping at Grams' brandy? People don't fall in love in three days."

"Nope. Only takes a minute." Grinning impishly, Violet began humming the Tavares tune.

Lifting her palms skyward and slapping her hands back to her side, Heather shook her head. Life was *not* like some oldies disco hit. There was no point in arguing. Her sister had simply lost her mind. Maybe it was being at the lake with Lucy singing and humming old matchmaking songs that had reverted Violet to her romantically delusional teenage years where good looks were confused for perfection and hormones for love. Maybe Jake was a nice guy, a really nice guy. Maybe he made Heather's heart thunder against her ribs with just a glance. And maybe she should find out what the heck was wrong with her grandfather and get her derriere back to the hospital where she belonged. Maybe.

# CHAPTER TEN

"**A**bout time you got back." Cindy looked up from the kitchen table. "We almost sent out a search party. Coffee's past cold."

Poppy looked over her cousin's shoulder. "Where's Jake?"

"He went home." Heather pulled out a chair and plopped down beside her cousins. "He didn't want to get in the way of our plans for the General."

"No," Callie snickered, "mustn't do that."

Heather frowned. "What's she laughing at?"

Standing closest to Callie, her sister Cindy elbowed her. "Nothing."

Nothing Heather's left foot.

Biting back a grin, Lily opened the oven door and pulled out a tray of fresh meringue cookies and set them beside another batch on the island. Spread out was an assembly line of sorts: eggs, chocolate shavings, powdered sugar, and at the end a finished plate of the wonderful meringue confections. "I almost burned the last batch thanks to you."

"Me?" Heather reached for one of the cookies.

"Lady and Sarge kept barking," Lily focused on moving the cookies from sheet to cooling rack, "so Callie went to go look."

"And of course," Cindy grinned, "I followed."

Cookie halfway to her mouth, Heather's stomach did a sudden somersault.

"And I shooed them all back inside." Poppy raised a cookie to Heather the way she'd toast with a glass of wine. "But it wasn't easy."

"We had to see who won." Cindy grabbed a cookie.

Heather didn't like the sound of that. "Won?"

Empty baking sheet in hand, Lily set it aside and starting separating egg yolks and whites, looked up to her cousin. "The bet of course. You didn't think you could get all romantic on us and not have folks taking bets. I mean seriously," she returned to cracking eggs, "it's better than speculating on the Kentucky Derby. Personally, I'm thinking this has potential for a triple crown win."

Heather wasn't sure she wanted to know how anything in her life could be related to a triple crown in horse racing, but then again she wasn't a believer in ignorance was bliss. "I give up. I'm not a horse. What are you talking about, Lily?"

"Well I'd say dancing in the moonlight definitely constitutes a win. I mean," Lily looked up at her sisters and cousins, "when was the last time any of you got to dance anywhere, never mind in the moonlight?"

Staring at Heather, everyone present grinned like Cheshire cats and shook their heads.

Lily started hand whipping the egg whites. "There you have your Kentucky Derby win."

"Oh for heaven's sake." Heather pulled a stool out from under the island with her foot, grabbed another cookie, and plopped heavily on the seat. She could tell this conversation was going to take lots of sugar. "Don't be ridiculous. It was just a silly dance. Y'all did it all the time when you were teenagers."

Cindy tapped the tip of her nose as if they were playing charades. "And you've touched on the magic words. When we were teenagers."

"Wait a minute." Violet waved her arms at everyone. "They were dancing?"

"Oh...yeah," Callie and Cindy echoed. Heather just looked up and nodded.

"I take one short walk to answer one phone call and I miss the one time my big sis has probably ever danced at the lake." Violet blew out a huffy breath of air and sank onto the seat beside her sister. "Not fair."

"Ohh," Callie reached for a cookie, "it gets better."

This time Heather's stomach did a triple flip. The puzzle pieces coming together and the picture coming into focus. *Crud.*

"Better?" Violet's brows dipped into a confused V.

"Oh, yeah." Cindy bit into the meringue and groaned with delight. "I suppose if I don't have anyone to suck face with these are a pretty darn good second place."

"Why do you think I'm baking on a Friday night?" Lily tossed her sister a frustrated glare. "I haven't been on a date in so long I don't think I can remember when it was. And I'm not joking."

"It was Alan Peterman, from the bank." Poppy poured herself a glass of water. "Two years ago at the Fourth of July barbecue."

Lily glanced at the ceiling, "Oh, yeah. Another one of Lucy's fix ups. Probably why I don't remember. And thank heaven he took that promotion in Cincinnati."

"Wait a minute," Violet cut in, waving her hands in front of her and spun to face her sister. "You kissed him?"

"The Preakness." Lily waved a meringue covered fork at Heather.

"Holy…" Violet grabbed a cookie, a clear sign of how distraught she was. The woman never touched anything that was mostly pure sugar. "And I missed it."

"You'll have to promise to tell us how the Belmont goes," Cindy stood and grabbed a drinking glass, "cause you'd better not be doing *that* on the Point."

"Shh." Poppy looked through the doorway to the parlor where her grandmother and Lucy were having a cup of tea together. "You don't want Lucy to hear. She'll start planning the wedding."

"Wedding?" Heather shoved to her feet. "Okay. Poke fun at Heather time is done."

Cindy swallowed a laugh. "Interesting choice of words."

"Grrr," Heather rumbled. "You do remember why we're all here tonight?"

"Yeah." Callie nodded with a smile. "Do you?"

"Of course I do. Which is why we've got to get moving. Did the General get his kolackys?"

All the cousins nodded

"Good. What about his Irish coffee?"

"That too," Cindy added.

"And," Callie waved her thumb over her shoulder at Poppy, "Sis asked him about his new friends on the internet, so he's all settled in and content on the veranda off the dining room."

Veranda? An enclosed three season area of the wrap around porch, the space had a clear view of the Point. Good thing Heather knew now that the General had discovered social media only a foreign invasion could drag his attention away. "Then here we go." She shot her arm straight out. "Ready?"

One by one a hand dropped onto the one underneath and the group chorused, *ready,* flinging their arms up in the air like a football team determined to mow down the opposition. Though she'd settle for getting a reading on heart rate and blood pressure. The rest of the battle she might need to bring in heavier hitters, but she'd save Grams until she needed her.

• • • •

"Those girls are up to something." Lucy strained to hear the conversation in the kitchen.

Fiona couldn't hold back the smile that tugged at her cheek. If raising three daughters had taught her anything, it was that no matter how old the girls grew, at some point or other they would always be up to something.

"It has to be something big to bring Heather here for this many days." Lucy continued rolling Fiona's yarn into a ball. "You don't suppose she's hiding a man, do you?"

This time Fiona laughed out right. "I don't think her pockets are that large." There was no point in feeding Lucy's matchmaking whims with what she'd seen from the parlor a short while ago.

"You know what I mean." Setting the large ball of yarn into the basket, Lucy grabbed the empty two liter pop bottle. "Something's up. I know it is. I can feel it in my left knee."

And folks said Fiona was the flighty one. If Lucy's left knee hurt it meant one thing, if her right knee hurt it meant something else. If her ears were ringing, it meant something different, and heaven forbid her palms started itching. Fiona couldn't keep track of which was what and she was pretty sure that neither could Lucy. Though this time, Lucy was right, she just didn't realize she was on the wrong track.

"All I know," Fiona spoke up, "is whatever brought Heather home, it's nice having so many of the girls here at once." It was kind of nice having a young man around the house too. Not that they didn't have plenty of men as guests, or friends coming to play cards in the evening, but having another man at the dinner table laughing and teasing like one of the family was a pleasant change.

"You notice the way Jake looks at Heather?" Lucy stabbed at the clear plastic bottle with a pair of scissors and cut off the top.

Fiona kept her gaze on her knitting needles, every time she dared to look up she'd lose a stitch. Besides, she didn't want to give anything away. "Can't say that I did." Well, maybe had she been closer she might have, but now wasn't the time to say anything. Not yet.

"Of all the boys that hung around here with the girls like moths chasing a flame, I remember Jake being one of the more responsible ones."

"Yes." Fiona couldn't argue. He'd been a good kid and when he'd come home from the Marines, he'd done a good job of taking care of his ailing parents.

"Kept my eye on him, making deliveries to Rebecca's cabin these weeks. Grew up good and strong."

Fiona nodded. She couldn't argue that point either.

"If you ask me, it's about time one of these girls showed some serious interest in a man. It's been too long since we've had little ones in this big old house." Lucy dropped the big ball in the base of the bottle.

Carefully pausing the interaction of the knitting needles, Fiona dropped the odd shaped blanket on her lap. "I must admit, it would do this heart good to see my girls happily settled with a good man they could grow old with, and little ones once again playing on the beach."

"Yes, sirree," Lucy waved a finger at her longtime employer, "and I think we've got ourselves a live possibility here. It just so happens I boxed up some supper leftovers for Jake. Think our Heather would be just the person to run them over to him so he'll have them for lunch tomorrow. Yes sirree, indeed. Time to reel that man in."

"Oh, Lucy," Fiona smiled and picked up the needles again, "it's not a fishing tournament. The girls will find the right man in due time. You just wait and see. Pretty soon, one by one, they all start finding their soul mates." Though she did like Jake. He had good strong roots going back to both sets of grandparents.

Lucy strung the end of the yarn through the open bottle top. "I suppose that's what happened with their mamas."

"Exactly. Rebecca then Virginia and right on their heels my Marissa found their men. Good men." Still, Fiona considered, maybe inviting Jake to another card game and then Sunday supper might not be a bad idea. After all, Heather might be a brilliant surgeon and loving granddaughter, but heaven help her, the art of romance did seem to escape her. Yes, the clacking of her needles picked up speed, cards and dinner were definitely in order. And maybe those leftovers weren't a half bad idea either.

• • • •

"Now isn't this a pretty picture." The General's gaze skipped from one granddaughter to the next.

Heather knew exactly how a raw recruit must have felt. "This will only take a few minutes." She reached for her grandfather's wrist only to have him yank it back with more force than she'd expected. And she had anticipated a good deal of resistance. Maybe she should have had Jake stick around.

"Now General," Cindy maneuvered herself to her grandfather's other side, "you know how much we love you."

"Yes." Sitting on the floor, Poppy rested her hand on the older man's knee. Her sparkling green eyes leveled with his, silently pleading her case.

For a few seconds, Heather spotted the softness in her grandfather's eyes. Not that she believed the General had a favorite, but it was fair to say his youngest grandchild's always sweet demeanor seemed to be his weakest link.

Unfortunately, the kink in his armor sealed up as quickly as it had opened. "You can show me how much you love me by believing me when I tell you I am perfectly fine."

"Okay." Heather crossed her arms. "Then why did you go see the doc?"

"Who told you that?"

"You did."

The General's bushy brows buckled together. Heather knew the exact second he remembered his slip on the phone the other day. "A checkup at my age is a perfectly normal thing."

"Then humor me." Heather put the stethoscope in her ears.

All she'd had time to do was blow her warm breath on the end before the General had patted Poppy on the head and pushed to his feet. "That will not be necessary, I am perfectly fine. I am also calling it a night."

"General." Callie positioned herself closer to Heather. "It will only take a minute, sir."

Flanked on Heather's other side and successfully blocking the General's exit, Violet lifted her chin and stared into her grandfather's eyes. "Please let Heather practice on you like she did when she was a kid."

Behind the General, Cindy almost spit with laughter. No doubt the visions of the buzz cut muscleman general, bigger than Goliath to all of his grandchildren, wrapped in layers and layers of toilet paper after having been bandaged by Heather flashed through her mind and everyone else's. Even the General's hardened stare seemed to soften.

The cousins had done their best to put forth a united front, but the second his gaze hardened again, Heather knew that stethoscope wasn't coming another inch closer to her grandfather's chest.

"Good night ladies." Easily maneuvering around Violet, with two dogs on his heels, the General marched out of the room.

A rhythmic chant of left, right, left, right played silently in Heather' head with the old man's every step. "I've only got a few more days. We're going to need a better plan."

Lily stepped out from behind Cindy. "Maybe next time I should try rum cake for dessert. With extra rum."

"Next time," Heather blew out a breath, "maybe we really should call in the SEALs for backup."

Cindy stood beside her. "Not sure that would help."

No, Heather had to agree. Jake was right. No military man wants to argue with a general. *Jake*. The mere mention of the man's name set her lips to humming again. And wasn't that a whole different problem she didn't need?

● ● ● ●

Living alone in the home he'd grown up in had never bothered Jake. Until now. Suddenly the house seemed very big—and very empty. Sitting alone at the kitchen table he stabbed at a piece of blueberry pie. His neighbor had baked it for him when he helped her till over the end of season soil in her vegetable garden. His mind wandered back through the years to times when the kitchen table was crowded with family friends. His mom loved company. In some ways she reminded him of Mrs. Hart. Oh, his mom was more practical and less worldly, but she loved fussing over and caring for people. After a couple of days at Hart House, he was beginning to realize he liked people too. Or maybe, one *people* in particular.

The ding from the doorbell snapped him out of his thoughts. Glancing up at the kitchen clock, it was an odd hour for visitors.

"Just a…" His words trailed off at the sight of Heather on his front porch. "Hi."

Stretching out her arm, she handed him a paper shopping bag. "Lucy sent leftovers from dinner tonight. She's convinced if you don't have them for lunch tomorrow you'll wither away."

"If only Lucy knew." He laughed and stepped away from the door. "Come on in. I was just having dessert."

"Oh well, I don't want to take up your time. It's late." Heather hesitated at the threshold, her gaze scanning the room.

"It's not that late. I'd love some company." She stepped into the house and he closed the door behind her. "Do you like blueberry pie? I have some apple too and there's probably a cherry in the freezer."

Her gaze continued to study the furnishings. "Um, yes I do, but I'm still full from dinner and Lily's desserts."

"I see. Well, let me put these in the refrigerator." He waved for her to follow him into the kitchen.

"I have to admit," she trailed after him, "this wasn't what I expected."

"Excuse me?" He kept an eye on her as he opened the refrigerator and shifted a few things around to make room.

"I was going to say the living room, but now your refrigerator is a bit of a surprise as well." Her forehead pleated in thought. "You didn't cook all this, did you?"

Closing the fridge door, he shook his head.

"And the doilies and blankets on the sofas and tables, those aren't your mother's, are they?"

He shook his head again.

Nodding, she turned to look at the living room. "Not much, huh?"

"Excuse me?"

"You told me that you don't help neighbors all that much." She waved her arm at the sofa and loveseat. One draped with the quilt Mrs. Hanson had given him last winter and the other with an afghan Mrs. Porter had knit. "I'm getting a different picture here."

Not that he had anything to hide, but pretty much only he and Tom, and the folks they helped, knew just how much he did for the elderly and veteran community. He was darn fortunate to have a successful business that allowed him time and affordable supplies to do his share giving back. "I may have helped out a bit more here or there."

One eyebrow shot up. "A bit?"

"A bit." He nodded.

Her gaze studied him long and hard. "Is the coffee still warm?"

"You bet." He could feel the smile pressing against his cheeks. "Sure I can't talk you into some pie?"

"Not unless you want to roll me out of here. Being around Lily, I've been in perpetual sugar overload." She watched him pour the black liquid into an old Bruins mug.

"How do you take it?"

"Regular."

He nodded, and quickly added milk and sugar before handing it off to her. "It's not as good as what Lucy makes, but it's a close second."

She wrapped her fingers around the mug. "Compared to what I'm used to I'm sure it'll be wonderful."

Rather than take a seat they stood side-by-side, backs to the counter. He liked standing close to her. Maybe a little too much. If only her life wasn't in another city.

"I understand why you do it."

He tightened his grip on his own mug. "I suppose you do. Fixing an old woman's kitchen sink or building a wheelchair ramp for a former Marine isn't quite the same as life-saving surgery, but the looks on their faces when I'm finished is worth everything."

"Don't sell yourself short." She raised her gaze from the mug to meet his. "What you do can be as much of a lifesaver as what I do."

His heart rate kicked up a notch. Memories of their earlier kiss urging his hands to slip around her and pull her close. The warmth in her eyes drew him in like the proverbial moth to a flame. He wasn't sure who shifted to face each other first, or when either of them had set their mugs on the counter. "Heather," he whispered.

"Jake." His name came out soft and low and completely irresistible.

Good, bad, or crazy idea, it didn't matter anymore. In a flash, he'd pulled her against him and his mouth brushed against hers. Slowly, softly—perfectly.

Her arms snaked around his neck, her fingertips dancing along his skin, and his heart slammed double time against his rib cage. How he wanted to pull her closer, tighter. Not even the ringing sound could bring him to let go of her.

*Ringing?*

The bell tone sounded again and she retreated a step, her hands slipping to his waist and sliding away. "I have to answer this."

His forehead dipped and he sucked in a steadying breath. "Of course."

Turning her back, she slipped out of reach and slowly made her way into the living room. "Dr. Preston here."

Breathing in and out slowly to still his heart, he didn't know whether to thank the person on the other end of the line for stopping him from doing something they'd both regret in the morning, or strangle them.

Her free hand pinching the bridge of her nose, she nodded and responded something he couldn't quite hear.

From her stiff stance, he had a feeling whatever was happening on the other end wasn't good and could very easily be a matter of life and death. The brutal reality of what this woman did for a living smacked him in the chest.

"I'll check in tomorrow." Heather blew out a sigh and slowly slid her phone into her back pocket.

"Something wrong?"

She sighed. "Maybe. I did a delicate surgery a few days ago. I left instructions to inform me of any changes. Heart rate and respiration are elevated. Could be nothing. But if it is, I'll be on my way back to Boston sooner than later."

"I see." For some inexplicable reason, pride bloomed deeper and stronger than if he'd been the one to save the patient's life.

"I should probably get going." She smiled tentatively.

Reluctantly, he bobbed his head. "Of course."

Sucking in one more deep breath, he flung the front door open, and stepped to one side.

Heather crossed onto the porch and turned to face him. "Goodnight."

"Night." He didn't dare move.

She took a step backward. "Will I see you tomorrow?"

He nodded. "Still have to paint."

"Oh, yes. That's right." Still smiling, she spun around and hurried off to her car.

At the sight of her car zipping away from the curb, an odd sense of loss took up residence in the pit of his stomach. He should probably get used to it. A few more days and she'd be hurrying off for good.

# CHAPTER ELEVEN

"Since there isn't anything that needs painting here at the shop," Tom looked from the painting supplies piled near the back door to his boss, "I'm guessing you're not sticking around this morning."

Jake's head whipped up from the last tidbit of paperwork he needed to complete before escaping for the day. "Davey will be here in about another half hour. Wants to put in some extra hours, see if he can get some more savings for next semester."

Tom nodded and Jake knew the man was thinking something else. Something he wasn't ready to say.

"Spit it out." Jake tossed the pen on the desk.

Lips pressed tightly in a thin line, Tom nodded more to himself than anyone in the room. "You know I'm as willing as the next guy to help a neighbor in need."

Jake dipped his chin in curt agreement. For as much as Tom occasionally razzed him over all the homemade casseroles in the freezer, the doilies covering every wooden surface at his house, and the knit blankets scattered and stored in every room and closet, Jake knew Tom had done his share of good-neighbor repairs not only in Lawford, but in surrounding communities as well. There were plenty of veterans who needed a leg up.

"Well," Tom continued, his hand clutching the back of his neck, "you've been out *helping* every day this week."

With another bob of his head Jake agreed and wished Tom would take the short cut to make his point. Jake had plans today with Dr. Preston that involved more than painting the bathroom wall.

"And I know this place is fully staffed, but don't you think you should maybe put in more than a token appearance?"

The question caught Jake completely off guard. He couldn't remember a single time when Tom had challenged him so solemnly. Yeah, once in a while Tom teased him, or joked with him, but there wasn't any hint of a gag line at the end of that question. Jake's knee-jerk reaction was to get in the guy's face about questioning how he ran his business, but the side of him who had served six years in a hell hole with this guy took a deep breath and a moment to consider before asking, "What aren't you saying?"

The hand that had been gripping his neck as though preventing his head from falling off, now ran roughly through his hair before his back straightened and he looked Jake dead in the eyes. "The way you've run out of here every day as though someone's life depended on it, as though your life depended on it, makes me think you are taking this do-gooder thing a bit too far. I know none of us see things the way we used to." He paused for a pensive breath. "There are pieces of us that we left over *there*, had to leave over there. And there are small parts of us that wonder every day why we're the ones who came home looking unscathed, but man, you don't have to prove anything to anyone."

Jake's mouth dropped open before his brain kicked into gear. "You think I'm on some kind of latent post-traumatic guilt trip?" Jake pushed to his feet. The honest fear and concern burning in Tom's eyes pricked a hole in the burst of fury that had risen in such a flash. Taking a step away from the desk, away from Tom's burning gaze, Jake sucked in a deep breath and collected his thoughts. "It's not like that. It's just been one little side job for the General."

Doubtful brows arched high over Tom's eyes. "For three days in a row?"

"The project had to be done in stages." Did he just whine?

Tom's gaze sharpened.

Yeah, Jake had whined. "What I meant was..." What had he meant? That he could have popped over for an hour or so each day but instead found reasons to hang out longer, to spend more time with Heather? To work on more than just the leaky bathroom?

"Wait a minute." Tom leaned forward and leveled his gaze with Jake once again. "There's something running through that thick skull of yours, but it's not survivor's guilt at all."

The loud ring tone burst from Jake's phone startling him back a step. Pulling it from his pocket, he answered without checking the caller name. "Hello?"

"I forgot to mention something last night."

There'd been no need to announce herself. Jake recognized the voice. "About what?"

"You were right. We need the Marine Corps to check that man's pulse."

A smile tugged at either side of his mouth. "That bad?"

"Oh, yeah. He won't walk within five feet of me this morning and even the Doc's nurse won't take my calls anymore."

Jake spun around and caught a glimpse of Tom watching him more closely than he would have expected. "What's the plan now?"

"That's just it. We don't have one. I know you were in the Corps. Got any ideas?"

"You can tell me more about what happened when I get there. Then maybe we can come up with a new plan."

Rather than step back as would have been appropriate when someone took a private call, Tom inched closer to Jake. His Marine Corps buddy could most likely hear Heather's every word as clearly as he could.

"Well, we'll have plenty of time," Heather continued. "The General is taking Grams to some specialty yarn shop just north of Boston. They won't be back till after supper."

"Really." Jake did a mental fist pump. The General couldn't have played into Jake's plans any better if Jake had actually told him what he'd hoped to do today. "I should be there in an hour or so. I'm almost finished with some paperwork and then I'll be heading in your direction."

"Thanks. See you soon."

His gaze lingered on the phone a second longer than it probably should have. When he looked up at Tom, the man was grinning like a drunken fool.

"I can't believe I was worried about you." Shaking his head, Tom took a step back. "It's a girl."

How was he supposed to answer that? Yes. Because it was. But it wasn't. No, what this came down to now wasn't about any girl. It was about the one who had been curled up on a porch chair reading when everyone else was having fun, the one who decided to save lives and did it, the one whose Mediterranean blue eyes could reel him in with one stubborn blink. Oh yeah, this was definitely about *the* girl.

• • • •

"How's it going, Jake?" Bobby, the manager of the Lawford Lake Marina slapped Jake on the shoulder.

"Great." He eyed the few toys in the small showroom. A couple of Jet Skis, a bass boat, and a sleek speedboat in bright cherry red that would make any man who loved the lake drool.

"That's a beaut, isn't she?"

"Certainly eye catching." Unable to resist, Jake ran his hand along the sleek hull.

Instincts like a shark, Bobby smelled his first whiff of blood. "You ready to stop renting and buy your own? She's got stern drive, ski bar, split bench rear with step through teak swim platform. This baby will leave butter smooth wakes." He raised his brows. "Slalom skiing is better than ever."

For a while there Jake had been stashing money away for some lake toys of his own, but through the years he'd had less time to spend playing and better uses for his money. Mrs. Norton's rotted siding came to mind and Jake pulled his hand away from the sweet ride. "Too nice a day not to spend some of it on the lake."

"That it is." In a silent statement, Bobby leaned against the shiny boat.

Maybe some day. In the meantime, "I was thinking of renting a couple of Jet Skis for the afternoon."

"Couple?" Bobby grinned. The Marina had been a family business since the first boat was brought to Lawford Lake. Technically Bobby's dad owned the business but as far as day to day activity went, it might as well have belonged to Bobby. "You holding out on me?"

First Tom now Bobby. The two had gone through twelve years of public school together. In a town as small as Lawford, and a county as rural as Beachum, even if you weren't in the same grade, everyone knew everyone. Including who dated who, who crushed on who, and who got lucky under the football bleachers. Except now they were all grown up and some things didn't need to be broadcast to the entire town. "Nope. Just too nice a day to spend alone."

Bobby raised one questioning brow. Whether or not the former high school football star believed him or not didn't really matter. Finally, when it was clear Jake had nothing else to add, Bobby nodded. "We've got a couple of new trade-ins that just went into the rental line. But I think I have a better idea."

"Great." Jake followed the man out the door and down one of the long wooden docks. When Bobby stopped and pointed, Jake knew what he had to do. Wasn't Heather going to be surprised?

• • • •

"I don't know." Violet sat in the middle of the front yard, soles of her feet touching, knees against the ground, palms raised to the sun. "I'm starting to think you're all wrong about this."

The thought had crossed Heather's mind. Not since the first day had she seen any sign of dizziness in the General, and the coughing seemed to have stopped, though she couldn't put her finger on how many days ago. Still none of it made sense. If he wasn't sick, why was he hiding from Doc Wilkins? Why wouldn't he let her even take his temperature? Something had to be up. "And if I'm not?"

"Yeah, well, that's the rub." Violet shot her legs out straight in front of her and leaned back on her elbows. "If you're not and we don't push it and something happens, well…"

"None of us will be able to live with ourselves." Heather looked down the Point and over the lake. Everything seemed so simple, easy when all you focused on was the serenity of Mother Nature at her best. Maybe she shouldn't pick on her sister quite so much. And maybe not every physical ailment had to be a matter of life and death. Still…

"What if we just sit down with Grams? I know you didn't want to worry her, but if she knows what's going on…?" Violet let the question hang.

"And if she doesn't?"

Her sister's brows bobbed up and down in what could only be described as a facial shrug.

"Oh, this is silly." Heather popped up from the grass and stood looking down at Violet. "I only have two more days."

Violet's serene expression crumpled in confusion.

"I have to be back to work on Monday." Even if Kyle and her other patients were doing well—in Kyle's case, in less than twenty four hours he'd gone from a concern to better than well—she had responsibilities. "It's practically a miracle I managed to clear my schedule for this many days as it is."

"True," her sister smiled up at her, "but it has been nice being back at the lake together. Would have been nice if Rose had made it up."

"And Iris and Zinnia. I haven't seen them in ages." Heather couldn't even calculate how long it had been.

"Hard to keep up with Iris. That family she works for does more traveling around the world than Phileas Fogg."

"Who?"

"You know, Pierce Brosnan."

Heather continued to stare expectantly.

"Phileas Fogg. *Around The World In Eighty Days*." When Heather's befuddled expression didn't clear, Violet shook her head. "Never mind Miss Nose-Always-In-A-Science-Book. Last I heard I think they're planning a trip to Thailand."

"Wow." Heather hadn't been more than a couple of hundred miles outside of Boston since, well, since Stanford. "Sounds amazing, I think, but I'm not sure I'd like that. I mean maybe if I got to—you know—perform surgery on poor kids or something."

"That's my sis." Violet grinned up at her. Not a hint of irony, only sheer pride.

Maybe some day she should look into that. Doctors Without Borders, or some other association, but in the meantime she had a different problem to fix much closer to home. "What are we going to do?"

"About Iris?"

"No," Heather huffed out her frustration. "I'm a grown woman. A recognized heart surgeon. Why won't the General just cooperate? Why is he making this so difficult for us?"

"Good question," the familiar baritone asked.

Rising fury with her stubborn grandfather crashed at the sight of

Jake approaching from... Heather scanned the driveway. "Where'd you come from?"

"Nice to see you too," he laughed.

Violet stuck her arm straight out toward the lake. "Thataway."

Shielding her eyes from the sun with her hand, Heather looked out. "Well you didn't rise from the fallows like Nessy."

A warm chuckle rumbled from deep in his chest. The sound gave her goose bumps. Now wasn't that ridiculous. Then he pinned his gaze on hers and the mind-scrambling connection from last night was back. If she thought last night's attraction was merely an illusion spawned from the romance of the moonlight and the music, or the proximity of confined quarters, she was very much mistaken. If the heat flooding every vein remembering the kitchen kiss was any indication, all that was needed for her to melt in place was a smile from Jake Harper. And what was she going to do about that?

• • • •

Everything in Jake wanted to reach out and run his fingers along the curve of Heather's jaw, the length of her neck, across her shoulders and then take her in his arms and hold her there until they were too old and feeble to stand on their own two feet.

He had two days until she returned to her world, and he was going to make darn sure that she never forgot them—or him. Holding out a large gym bag, he held the smile that came so easily. "You'll want to go put this on."

She accepted the bag but kept her gaze on him. "You still haven't told me where you came from." His grin stretched wider across his face. "Ah, that's a secret." He handed Violet a similar bag.

"Ooh, I like surprises." Violet unzipped the bag.

At the same time Violet pulled out the contents of her bag, Heather dangled the dark gray suit that had been in hers. "What is this?"

"I'd have thought it was obvious. A wet suit."

"Yes," Heather chuckled. "I know that, but why are you giving this to me?"

"Mostly because I don't want any arguments about the lake

giving you hypothermia."

"Oh, no." She shook her head. "I am not, I repeat not, swimming in that thing this time of year."

Violet looked up. "She may have a point, buddy."

"Did I say anything about swimming?"

"Actually," Heather let the hand holding the suit fall to her side "you haven't said much of anything that makes sense."

"You told me you'd never danced on the beach before."

Her cheeks tinged a pretty shade of pale pink.

"I think I hear Lucy calling me." Violet jumped to her feet.

"No." Jake forced himself to tear his gaze away from Heather. "Stay, this is for all of us."

Violet stopped, but she had that look of a deer about to dart across the road.

He returned his attention to Heather. "And that you didn't know how to water ski."

Beautiful blue eyes widened with understanding and luscious pink lips that he'd love to kiss again, only this time for hours, formed a perfect O.

"I thought now was as good a time as any." He had to resist a ridiculous urge to dig his toe into the sand and cross his fingers behind his back.

From the corner of his eye he saw Violet shift her gaze from him to her sister before nodding. "I think it's a great idea, but I already know how to water ski and I really do think I hear Lucy." And just like that she darted up the hill and across the drive.

"Even in the summer the water is never really warm. By now it has to be freezing," Heather muttered.

He didn't let his smile fade. "Not really, but that's what the suit is for."

Staring down at the suit in her hand, she heaved in such a deep breath, he could see her chest expand and release the air in a soft whoosh.

"Bobby at the Marina loaned me his personal boat." He hadn't realized how desperately he wanted her to say yes. To be the one to bring more fun into her life.

She looked over his shoulder to the lake.

"It's tied up. Go on inside. Change into a swimsuit and let's give this a shot."

Clutching the wet suit to her chest, she sucked in a long breath and bobbed her head. "Let's." Then, grinning like a teenager on summer break, she spun around and ran up the hill after her sister.

Jake had to take in an equally long deep breath to slow his racing heart. If luck and the grace of God were on his side, maybe this wouldn't be the only thing she'd be willing to give a shot.

• • • •

Bolting up the porch steps two at a time, Heather couldn't get inside Hart House fast enough to change. In such a hurry, she almost didn't see her grandmother knitting in her favorite rocker. "Grams, I thought you were going to the yarn store?"

"Just waiting on your grandfather to get off the computer chat." The woman didn't look up. "Where's the fire, dear?"

"Oh, I'm uh," she glanced down the hill to Jake by the edge of the Point and felt a smile rise up from her heart and take over her face, "going water skiing."

Keeping her eyes on the blanket that seemed to have doubled in size and distortion since a few days ago, her grandmother smiled. "That's nice, dear."

Nice? Was it? She looked to the water again. Yes, yes it was. Leaning over, Heather threw her arms around this pleasant, kind—and in her own way—always supportive woman. "Love you, Grams."

Carefully setting the needles down on her lap, Grams raised one arm to squeeze her back. "Love you too." This time she looked Heather in the eye and Heather had the feeling her grandmother knew so much more than she let on.

In record speed, Heather was on the boat in an old swimsuit that hadn't seen the light of day in years, covered by the wet suit that fit surprisingly well, and listening carefully to every word Jake said, even if most of it was going in one ear and out the other. After all, how was anyone supposed to process words when the speaker wore a skintight suit that showed every well-toned muscle?

"You think you got that?"

Heather blinked. Oh. Instructions. "Yes." She smiled.

"Good." He gave her a thumbs up. "Now for driving the boat."

She blinked again. "Driving?"

"Yes. I'm going to go in first. This way you can see how I do it. Granted, it's not the same watching but it can give you a visual to the instructions before you go in yourself."

"I see." Though she didn't really. Part of her felt as though someone was telling her how to perform heart surgery, then saying watch me, knowing the next thing would be her turn. But this wasn't surgery. It was sport. And though she'd never been an athlete, how hard could it be?"

"Now," he said, standing behind her, his arms around her sides, one on the steering wheel, one on the throttle. "You don't want to just ram it up or the person on the end of the rope will go face first into the water."

She nodded. Made sense. Physics classes on velocity and motion came to mind.

"You want to ease her into it." He pushed the handle up. "Nice and easy."

Jake might have been talking about the boat and the lake and waterskiing, but she was getting goose bumps all over again.

"You try it."

Smiling up at him, she bobbed her head, and then faced forward, did exactly as he'd showed her.

"Good, very good." He slapped her a high five and they eased the boat to a stop. "Okay. Let's get ready to go."

With almost choreographed ease, they moved back and forth on the sleek boat. Everything in place, Jake went over the side, sank under the water and came up shaking his head like a wet sheepdog.

"You okay?" she asked.

"You were right."

"I was?"

A grin spread from one side of his face to the other. "Too cold for skinny dipping."

Good thing she had a wet suit on because she was pretty sure she was blushing from her head to her toes. She slid his skis over the edge into the water one at a time, watching how easy Jake made putting them on look. Once he was all set, she gradually drove the boat forward as instructed, keeping an eye ahead at the wide open—and at this time of year—empty lake, before daring to look back over her shoulder.

Raising a thumbs up, he let her know he was ready to go.

"Nice and easy," she mumbled and pushed the throttle forward.

Behind her she saw Jake crouch low to the surface and slowly rise up like a phoenix from the ashes. Looking back and forth, the wind whipping at her face, the water sluicing along the sides of the sleek boat, and Jake sliding from side to side in the boats wake, she couldn't remember having more fun.

When his arms released the rope and he slowly sank into the water, her heart skipped a beat before she realized that's how it's supposed to happen. Carefully circling around she slowed, not too far, but not too close to him, and stopped. "Textbook perfect," she shouted.

Jake threw his head back with laughter. "Okay, your turn."

Back on board, he switched out his skis for hers and helped her into the water. She was both nervous and excited and didn't know whether to dive in or pass out.

"You'll do great. Remember, don't force it. Just let the water help you stand."

Nodding, she jumped over the edge and plunged under the icy water. Definitely wet suit weather. Carefully placing her foot into the rubber inserts, she slid on the first, then second ski, repeating to herself, "Nice and easy."

First attempt was neither nice nor easy. She face-planted into the water and swallowed at least half the lake. Okay, maybe not quite half.

"Are you okay?" The look of near panic on his face had her smile through the cough.

"Yes. Let's do it again."

That face splitting grin returned. "You got it."

It took two more tries before she found herself on her feet and hooting at the wind. How had she never done this before? No wonder all the kids loved being on the lake. As a small child she'd loved swimming, but she loved reading books and the world they took her to just as much. She wasn't so sure she would have so easily turned her nose up at waterskiing if she'd ever actually tried it. A good reason to spend more time on the lake next summer.

Who was she kidding? She didn't need waterskiing to make her want to come to the lake. The man in front of her, stepping out of the dripping wet suit and smiling at her as though she held the moon in her hand, was all the reason she needed to return more often. The thought of not coming back, not seeing him for years again, hurt more than it should. Reminiscent of the pain she'd felt when she'd lost her first patient. How could that be?

# CHAPTER TWELVE

"Well it's awfully nice having you with us for dinner and cards twice this week." Mrs. Hart looked up at Jake from her seat in the rocker.

Tonight Lily paired up with Jake, most likely in an effort to save him from the General's censure. Ralph, the neighbor and staple at the Hart card games, partnered with the General. That left Floyd the only man at the merry widows table with Louise Franklin from the drugstore, Thelma Carson from the antique store and Heather sitting in for Nadine Baker, the widows' ringleader home with a cold.

"Hope you plan to make this a habit," Fiona Hart smiled.

Smiling in her direction, Jake settled for a simple, "Thank you, ma'am."

"Floyd, if you don't start paying better attention to trump I'm going to partner up with Jake." Louise winked at him. "About time we had some decent eye candy at the tables."

Lily smothered a smile and kicked Jake under the table. "Your turn."

"Oh." He looked at the cards in his hand and realized between the ruckus from the old card players and stealing glimpses of Heather, he didn't have a clue what had been played. When all else failed, second hand low third hand high, and he was pretty confident Lily had dealt so he was second hand low and played his three of clubs.

Flexing his fingers and shaking his head, Ralph held back a cough and Jake wondered if the man was getting sick or if playing that card had been a mistake. From how the whites around Lily's eyes widened, he was absolutely positive he'd made a mistake.

Lily blew out a frustrated breath. "I may take Mrs. Franklin up on her offer to trade partners. Clubs are trump and I didn't deal."

"And that's why he's yours tonight." The General laid down a lowly four of clubs and scooped up the trick.

"I bet the boy's in love," Floyd said over his shoulder. "My bet is on that pretty new waitress at Mabel's."

"Nah," Ralph muttered, shook his free hand then flexed his fingers—his left hand—before playing the next card. "A strong, good-looking guy like him, he's probably got his eye on Kathy from the Soak and Spin."

A sixth sense that had come in handy more than once pricked at the back of Jake's neck.

Louise frowned. "Now why would he like Kathy from the Laundromat over the new waitress?"

Jake kept a careful eye on Ralph while wondering if he should point out that *he* was right here. Playing another card, he glanced briefly to the table beside him. As far as he was concerned, there wasn't anyone in or out of town that compared to Heather Preston.

"Of course, there's no shortage of nice girls in this town. Right, Lily?" Louise winked at Jake's partner.

"Don't look at me. I could never marry a man who cannot remember trump," Lily teased through a smile.

Jake avoided meeting Heather's gaze and giving his feelings away. Instead, he turned to Lucy coming through the door with a tray of cool drinks. "Actually, I'm still holding out for Lucy. She had me years ago with her French toast casserole."

"That's me." Lucy burst out laughing. "Cougar extraordinaire."

All players at both tables joined in the laughter. Only Ralph's laugh shifted to another stifled cough as he played the next card. His left hand steady as a rock, at least he'd stopped the flexing.

"You guys seem to be having too much fun without me." Callie came through the screen door and plopped in the seat next to her grandmother. "Next time the principal asks me if I can take on the girls' JV basketball team on top of the varsity team, someone just shoot me. I'm exhausted."

"Nonsense." Her grandmother didn't look up from her knitting. "You love the game and the girls."

"True." The smile slipped from Callie's face, her expression contorting as her head tipped sideways staring at the sprawling yarnwork. "I thought you were making a baby blanket."

Lily snorted a stifled laugh.

"No, I got a little carried away. It's now a blanket for your mother," Mrs. Hart answered sweetly.

"A little," Ralph muttered and Louise Franklin skewered him with a tight-lipped glare.

"Coach Callie," a smiling teen with long blonde hair in a pony tail popped her head in the screen door, "do you want us to set up on the Point or the sand?"

"The sand. Give me five minutes and I'll be right there."

The girl nodded, then turned to the other adults. "Evening General Hart, Mrs. Hart. Thanks for letting us have our marshmallow roast."

Fiona Hart lifted her gaze to meet the young girl's. "Any time, Susie."

Growing up, it had always marveled Jake how every adult in town had known every kid's name, who their mother and father were, what mischief they might be creating or what achievements they'd reached. Apparently some things never changed.

"You win again?" the General asked.

"Yes, sir," the girl beamed. "Overtook them by three points just before halftime and never lost control of the court again. We're heading to semi finals."

"Well," the General grinned at the excited teen, "that sounds like reason enough to celebrate to me."

"Coach Callie is the best." The blonde's smile held strong.

"You guys put in the hard work. That's what did it." Callie pushed to her feet. Brushing off her exhaustion, she slapped her hands and rubbed them together vigorously. "We're going to roast marshmallows tonight."

"Sounds like I'd better whip up some of my hot chocolate for those marshmallows." Lucy smiled at the still grinning girl in the doorway. "Maybe add some graham crackers and chocolate bars too."

"Sweet!" Susie did a fist pump.

Mrs. Hart set her knitting down beside her and looked to Lucy. "If the whole team is here, you'll need some help."

"Since when can I not handle a beachfront of teens?"

A booming laugh came from the General. "She's got you there."

Rolling her eyes, Fiona Hart walked past her husband and patted his shoulder. "An extra pair of hands in the kitchen never hurt.

Especially with hot drinks."

"Of course." The General reached up and squeezed her hand before letting go and facing the teen still in the doorway. "What do you think of having the team here tomorrow afternoon for a nice barbecue? I'll put out the horseshoes and the volleyball net and we'll celebrate in style."

"Yes!" Susie gave out another joyous cry. Had Jake ever had that much energy?

"All right." Callie nudged Susie out the door. "Let's get the fire started, and everyone can work out who's coming tomorrow and let my grandmother know."

Susie hurried toward the lake, shooting questions at Callie. *Do you think he'll let us use the paddle boats? Oh I hope it's not too cold.* Slowly their voices disappeared into the distance. Jake understood their excitement. Nothing went better with teenage years than bonfires on the sand, games on the Point, and all the food you could eat.

"Let's go, Lucy." Fiona Hart followed the housekeeper inside.

"I could use a change of luck." Lily skewered him with a pointed glare. "I think I'll help Grams and Lucy for a minute."

"Good idea." Heather and the remaining card playing ladies stood and followed Lucy and Mrs. Hart into the house.

"I suppose." Ralph gathered the cards in front of him and paused to flex his fingers and rub his forearm.

Jake cut off the rest of his thought. "You feeling okay, Ralph?"

"Of course. Why wouldn't I be?"

"You seem to have hurt your hand." Right about now, Jake wished Heather had stayed with the men and could get a look at Ralph.

"Just my arthritis kicking in. As I was saying," Ralph continued, "maybe we should go see if the women need a hand?"

"Good idea, Ralph." Jake shoved to his feet. "Let's go."

"Me?" the older man's eyes widened. "I was thinking you."

Jake nodded. If Mohammed wouldn't go the mountain, Jake would just have to bring the mountain—or Heather—to Ralph

• • • •

"I'd better get a head count." Lucy spun on her heel. "Be right back."

"You two look awfully cute." Lily pulled a couple of saucepans from under the sink.

"Are we going there again?" Gallon of milk in hand, Heather shoved the fridge door closed.

Lily waved her free hand in the air. "Just making an observation."

"Did I miss something?" One of the merry widows asked, setting Styrofoam cups on the counter.

"You're not the only one." The other woman counted out napkins.

"All I meant was…" Staring at the doorway, Lily's words fell off.

"If I were a little bit more insecure, I'd think you were talking about me." Jake crossed the threshold and strode straight for Heather. "I'm worried about Ralph."

"Ralph?" She set the milk container on the counter by the stove. "Why?"

"Something about the way he keeps flexing his left hand. I keep remembering that story you told me."

"What story?" Lily looked up.

"Heather!" Lucy's voice came screeching from the front hall.

"Uh oh." The two card playing women echoed.

Already at the doorway, Heather stopped at the sight of Lucy rushing through the living room. "Hurry. I think he's having a heart attack."

She didn't have to ask who. "Jake. Run upstairs. I've got my medical bag in my room."

He nodded and bolted up the stairs two at a time.

The same two teens stood beside Floyd and her grandfather. She'd need to talk to him about having a defibrillator on hand.

Susie turned and backing away, her face pale, nearly cried. "We came to help Lucy with the hot chocolate. We've already called 911."

The lake emergency services covered a lot of territory. Sometimes things worked out better than others. "Excuse me," she mumbled, hurrying past the General and kneeling beside her cousin, another young teen she didn't recognize and Ralph.

Callie, arms locked, was pumping on Ralph's chest. "You wanna step in and I'll take over for Jimmy?"

Heather glanced at the young man looking a bit green about the gills but focused on blowing measured breaths into Ralph's lungs. "Shift."

Callie moved to kneel at Ralph's head. A siren sounded in the distance growing louder. "Thank you, Lord."

Taking a second to check for any signs of breath or heart beat, Heather said a silent prayer and took over where her cousin had left off.

A blaring siren came to a screeching silence and the two sets of thundering footsteps sounded like an army of angels to Heather. Within seconds the defibrillator was set up, oxygen on the ready. "Clear!" she shouted.

Most everyone on the porch jolted with Ralph.

"Again." Watching the meter rise, years of Ralph grumbling over hooligans on the trains and bad card players flashed through her mind as easily as oxygen passed through her lungs. "Clear!"

Another jolt and he was back in sinus rhythm.

She and everyone around her expelled a unified relieved breath. Moving like a well practiced team the EMT's had Ralph on the gurney ready for transport, Heather hurrying alongside.

"Want me to drive you to the hospital?" Jake asked.

So focused on Ralph, she hadn't noticed Jake rushing beside her. Something inside went warm and fuzzy that he didn't ask if she would go with him but whether she needed a ride. She shook her head. "I'll ride in the ambulance."

He nodded. "I'll meet you there."

"No." She grabbed the handle and hefted herself inside before turning to face him. "I'm not sure how long I'll be there. Please stay and make sure everyone's okay. I love my grandfather but he can be a bit..."

"Military." The way his eyes studied her face and the muscles along his jaw line tightened, she thought he might object, but heaving a deep sigh, he nodded. "Got it covered. Keep us posted."

Violet came running up to them, dangling keys, paused long enough to huff out, "I'll follow. Make sure you have a ride home," then flew past them and climbed into the driver side of her old Honda.

"Count on me." Jake gave her a reassuring smile as the ambulance door slammed shut and she knew that counting on him might come a little too easily.

• • • •

Not till the taillights of the ambulance disappeared up the hill did Jake turn to the General standing beside him.

"Tomorrow isn't promised," the older man muttered.

"No, but if you have to count on anyone, I'd count on Heather."

"You got that right." The General sighed.

"Yes, sir." Jake could imagine too well the thoughts running through the retired general's mind. He, like Jake, had no doubt seen countless buddies hauled off behind the closed doors of an emergency vehicle and only time would tell if they would see them again. At least this time he could rest assured that Ralph couldn't be in better hands. Seemed saving lives came as naturally to Heather as breathing.

Fiona Hart had sidled up beside her husband, her arm casually slipping around his waist. A silent comfort that had come from years of standing as one. For the first time that Jake could remember, the General looked old. Heather must have anticipated the toll this would take on him.

Turning, he was almost surprised to see everyone including the basketball team had gathered behind them, stunned.

"Is he going to be all right?" Susie asked softly.

"He got the best care he could as fast as possible." Not only did Ralph have an experienced cardiologist on hand, but Callie had been on the job before Heather could reach Ralph. Putting on the reassuring smile that Heather would have wanted, he looked to Callie. "What do you think if we get that hot chocolate and wait on the beach for an update?"

Callie looked from her grandfather to her students, then slowly nodded. "Yeah, I think being able to process what happened together would be a good idea."

Following Callie and her students, Jake paused and glanced one last time at the empty road where the ambulance had been. Who was he kidding? Nothing would be the same once Heather returned to her world. A world that needed her as much as he did.

His mind drifted to earlier in the day. Heather, her smile intact, and her eyes sparkling from a day experiencing the lake to its fullest. The sheer joy on her face. Thoughts of how to keep the twinkle in her eyes rattled around in his mind. There was still one more thing he could do before she returned to her life in Boston. One more memory to hang on to.

● ● ● ●

For the first time since Heather had marched through the double doors of the ER, she could breathe easy.

"You're not smiling, but you're not frowning so I'm going to guess things could be worse." Violet stood in the center of the waiting room.

"He should be fine." As heart attacks went, it could most definitely have been worse.

"You look beat."

Now that the adrenaline rush was over, she was feeling the drop in energy. Not an attending physician at the small local hospital, she hadn't expected to be allowed into the ER with the patient. Apparently there wasn't a citizen within a hundred miles of Hart Land who didn't know about the General's granddaughter, the cardiac surgeon. By the time she'd hopped off the back of the ambulance, word had spread that she was coming in with the victim. From the few comments she'd managed to glean, according to her grandfather, she pretty much walked on water. Too bad that wasn't true; it could come in pretty handy in her line of work.

Palms flat on the small of her back, she twisted left, then right, before straightening. "They were a bit short handed." Not that the ER doctor couldn't handle caring for Ralph, but the on call cardiologist was delayed getting to the hospital. Since she could recognize a harmless anomaly in the test results as the mark of a more serious problem—or in this case lack of one—as easily as reading an eye chart with 20/20 vision, she casually pointed out what was obvious to her. "Without the staff cardiologist here there was a good chance

Ralph would have been transported to a larger hospital."

"But not this time?"

Heather shook her head. "I spoke with the staff cardiologist, he'll be here within an hour. Ralph will have to undergo some tests and they'll monitor him carefully but my money is on Ralph. He's a tough old goat."

"Good." Violet smiled.

The double doors swung wide again and the bed with a groggy but awake Ralph pushed past her.

"I hear you saved my day."

"You should be resting," Heather said softly, taking his hand in hers and squeezing before letting go.

"You heard the doctor." The orderly pushed the bed around the corner to the elevator bays.

Violet stepped around her sister and raised her hand to cup her mouth. "And don't go pinching all the nurses."

Neither could hear what Ralph answered, but the burst of laughter from the orderly pushing him into the elevator let them know the old coot still had his sense of humor.

"Thank you again." Stifling a yawn and cradling a chart against his chest, the ER doctor came to a stop at Heather's side. "Glad we didn't need to transport him to a larger facility," he hefted a lazy shoulder in a tired shrug, "but there isn't a doctor between here and Boston with better credentials than yours. You should follow your own advice. Go home to your family. Get some rest. We've got it covered."

"Thank you. I'll wait a bit till he's settled in his room and pop in to say goodbye."

The doctor nodded. "Fair enough. And for the record, if you ever want to leave one of the most prestigious hospitals in the country and stop performing groundbreaking surgeries," he shook his head and smothered a chuckle, "we're always in need of a good doctor."

She smiled back at him. "I'll keep that in mind."

"You do that." With a casual wave to both Heather and Violet, he turned and made his way back through the double doors.

"Wonder if he's single?" Violet pondered out loud. "No ring."

Heather chuckled. "I didn't ask."

"You wouldn't be interested anyhow. You've got Jake."

"I don't *have* anyone." Though she did want very badly to hear his voice, and had the phone to her ear before she noticed the wry grin on her sister's face. "I need to catch everyone up on what's going on."

"Sure you do." Violet's grin widened.

"Hello." The sound of his voice smoothed over her raw nerves. "I was hoping to hear good news sooner than later."

"He's going to be fine. No serious blockage."

"Thank heaven," his tone dripped with relief. "Everyone's doing their best to stay positive, but you can feel the worry in the air. "

"Go ahead and let folks know he's on his way to a room. Will probably remain in the hospital for a few days, but the merry widows can start lining up the casserole entourage."

Jake burst into laughter. "Too late. Already started. Lucy is first on the list with her King Ranch casserole."

"I should have known." Heather could hear the rumbling of teen voices spewing questions at Jake: Who's on the phone? Is it about Ralph? How is he?

"Hang on," he muttered, either to her or the teens she wasn't sure. "Listen," he must have walked away from the group because the chatter had dimmed, "I need to give an update and help Callie ship the kids off. A few parents are here. No one wanted to leave without news."

"I'm not surprised." Lawford really was an anomaly in modern times. "Go ahead. I'll talk to you tomorrow."

"Will do. And Heather…"

"Yeah?"

"You were amazing."

Too tired to argue she'd only done what Callie had done, she nodded to no one. "Good night."

"Good night." She turned to see Violet grinning.

"For a smart doctor," Violet shook her head, "you really do have a lot to learn. Let's go home. Maybe a good night's sleep will knock some sense into you."

Without a word Heather followed her sister, but she doubted seriously that a lack of sleep had anything to do with what had her out of sorts at the moment.

# CHAPTER THIRTEEN

"You're up awfully early." Lucy stood at the sink peeling potatoes.

Heather had given up on getting a decent night's sleep. After a full day of cavorting on the lake—and didn't that sound nice—supper with a troop of matchmaking family, an evening of card playing, a medical emergency, and then staying late at the hospital with Ralph, all sorts of things had been scrambling around in her mind. Questions, feelings, and not nearly enough answers.

"Coffee's fresh." Lucy waved at the pot.

"Thanks." It was going to be hard going back to the sludge the hospital called coffee. Pot in hand, Heather blinked. A lot of things were going to be hard about going back to the hospital. Leaving Jake Harper behind was rapidly rising to the top of the list.

"I'll be putting breakfast out for everyone soon. You want to eat early?"

Heather shook her head. "I'll wait for the others."

Lucy nodded and went back to peeling potatoes. "It's always nice when Callie's students come to the lake. Doesn't happen often this time of year but the laughter keeps us all young. Especially after that scare with Ralph last night. A simple day at the lake will be good for everyone."

"Mm." Heather took a sip of the coffee. Lucy had a point in one way for sure – there was always something magical about the lake. That's probably all this fluttering in her stomach was about. The lake. When she returned home, to her routine, her life, Jake Harper would barely be a memory.

The figment of her memory suddenly stood before her. "Morning."

For a few seconds she actually thought she was hallucinating. At least until Lucy put down the peeler and wiped her hands on her apron.

"The General said to tell you he'll be down in a minute. Have you had breakfast yet?"

His cheeks pinkened. "No, ma'am. Didn't want to be late."

What was that all about?

Puppy nails clacking on the wooden floors announced the arrival of Lady and Sarge.

"Good morning fella." Jake leaned over to pet Lady who had sat in front of him, tail wagging. He'd gotten in only a short scratch before she moved her nose and nudging his hand out from over her, and gave him a big slobbery lick.

"Guess you must be okay." The General turned the corner into the kitchen. "Lady's rather fussy. Doesn't lick just anybody."

"'Specially men," Lucy chimed in.

"What about men?" Violet came into the room a few feet behind her grandfather.

Scratching Sarge behind the ear, Heather looked up. "Apparently Lady is particular about who she keeps company with."

Violet shrugged and reached for the coffee pot. "I'm starved."

"Table is set. Violet, you grab the pancakes in the top oven. Heather, the bacon and eggs are in the warmer."

"Aren't we waiting for Grams?"

"Grams," Fiona Hart floated into the room, wearing a nearly floor length striped broom skirt and a bright peasant top, "is here."

"What shall I carry?" Jake asked.

Lucy lit up as though he'd announced she was the new Miss America. "We've got it all covered. You just go on inside and make yourself at home."

"Yes, ma'am." He turned and sidled up beside Heather. "You sleep well?"

"Not really."

"Me neither."

She stopped short and spun to look at him.

"Sometimes sleep is overrated." Something in his tone told her his comment had nothing to do with last night's excitement and everything to do with the questions batting around in her mind. He reached around her and retrieved the platter of eggs. "Let me."

"Thanks." She could carry the platter fine, but the way he looked at her as though he could read her heart and soul would have had her turning over anything he asked for.

The dogs did their underfoot routine and once again Heather and Jake found themselves sitting side by side. This time Heather wanted to lean over and thank the pups.

"Jake and I are going to set up the volleyball net and rake the bocce court."

"So we're going ahead with the plans for the day?" Heather asked.

"Yes. Despite last night's shake up, the plans are solid. The children deserve a little celebration."

Heather was happy to see her grandfather reporting for duty. So to speak.

"Then," he continued, "we'll head out to the marina and pick up the paddle boats."

"Isn't it a little late in the season for that?" Violet asked.

The General nodded. "It is. We took them out of the water last month, but the kids enjoy it so much and the weather's been exceptionally warm the last few days."

Last night's scare had Heather even more uneasy about her own grandfather's health. Considered the ticking clock until her return home for her to finally uncover the truth, she turned to face Jake.

He gave her a curt nod, almost as if he knew what she was considering. Could it be they really did read each other so well, or was all this simply wishful thinking?

Grinning broadly, the General took a seat at the table. "It's going to be an outstanding day."

The prospect of a houseful of teens, no matter recent circumstances, seemed to have him in an especially good mood. Now that she had Jake's support, there was no better time than the present to tackle her grandfather again.

"Excuse me a minute." Heather stepped away from the table and hurried upstairs. Retrieving what she needed from her room, she hurried back down the stairs and slipped quietly into the dining room.

"Don't think I can't see you skulking about, young lady. I didn't get my stripes by not knowing what was going on around me." Buttering his toast, her grandfather didn't even bother to turn in her direction. It was like the man actually had eyes in the back of his head.

"General, this will only take a minute." Or twenty.

"Nonsense." He pushed to stand. "We have a barbecue to prepare for. No time for anything else."

"Enough," Heather barked. "This isn't the Marine Corps. I am not a rough recruit and you are not my superior officer."

"I'm your grandfather." His tone took on that military gruffness.

She came toe to toe with the stubborn old man. "And I am Doctor Heather Preston. Granddaughter of General Harold F. Hart. Now sit!"

Much to her surprise and everyone else in the room, the General dropped into the chair behind him.

"Now roll up your sleeve."

"Never, have I—"

"Sleeve," she practically growled.

Stethoscope on his arm, Heather listened and watched the secondhand on the wall clock circle around. She listened to his chest as he breathed in and out. Frowning, she took his pulse at his wrist and then did the same at his neck.

The tension in the room grew as thick as the humidity in August.

Shaking her head, she let go of his hand.

"How long have you had the murmur?"

The General shrugged. "It's nothing."

"Murmur," multiple voices mumbled in varied ranges of concern.

Looking at her family, she shook her head. "It's also called an innocent murmur. It doesn't affect anything. People can have one their entire lives and still live to be a hundred. None of the things I've seen would have been caused by that and everything else is within normal range. I don't understand it."

"I told you." He made a show of undoing his sleeve. "I'm fine."

"But the cough. The dizziness. The naps." She whirled to face her grandmother. "And giving up cigars and french fries?"

Fiona Hart smiled at her eldest grandchild. "So that's what this is all about."

Without saying a word, like a child caught with their hand in the cookie jar, Heather nodded.

Fiona gave her husband a look very similar to the one Heather had used when she finally got the man to cooperate.

The General snorted, before sighing. "All right. A few months ago I went in for a regular check up. Found myself getting confused, tired."

"And?" Heather asked.

"Turns out my blood pressure *was* a little high."

"Harold," his wife enunciated very clearly.

"220 over 145."

"Oh, General." Heather reached for the blood pressure cuff again.

"You can put that down. I got the lecture on cigars, salt, fats, fried foods, exercise. You know the drill."

Heather nodded.

"He gave me some pills—"

"That he didn't like taking," Grams added.

"And then Jim Parker had a stroke." The General paused to look at all the faces in the room. "He's fifteen years younger than me."

Grams patted her husband's knee and flashed a prideful grin at her granddaughters. "Four weeks later, your grandfather had lost ten pounds—"

Violet bobbed her head. "You do look pretty good of late."

"And his blood pressure is down to 130 over 80 and has been holding steady for months now," her grandmother continued.

"But the dizzy spells, the tiredness." Heather waved an arm from her grandmother to the General. "Those are all symptoms of high blood pressure."

The General nodded. "And fluid in the middle ear."

Clearing her throat loudly, Grams stared pointedly at her husband.

"I've developed allergies," he added.

"Allergies?" a few voices muttered.

The General reached into his pocket and handed Heather a bottle of pills. Sure enough, the prescription medicine was indeed used to reduce fluid in the ear, which would explain his symptoms.

Tenderness shone in his eyes, his hand dropped to her arm, and his voice came out so low and melodic she almost couldn't hear him. "From one little phone call you knew something was wrong. Best darn doctor I've ever known." As if realizing he was getting all mushy on her, he snatched his hand back, pushed away from the table, stood ramrod straight and groused for every person in the room to hear, "We have guests coming. Let's get cracking."

One by one the family jumped to attention and carrying their empty plates, filed into the kitchen. At the doorway, Jake slowed and turned to Heather. "I'm glad it's not serious."

"Me too, as long as he follows doctor's orders." Staring at the empty doorway the General had walked through, she couldn't decide why she didn't feel any better. "He's always complaining that I'm not here. That nothing is as important as family. Last night, today, that really hit home."

"He brags about you to everyone who will listen. He's very proud of you." To her surprise, Jake leaned in and gave her the tenderest of pecks on the lip. "And I love how the feeling is mutual." Without waiting for her response, he spun about and followed the others out of the room.

*Love.* The word kept her momentarily frozen in place. It wasn't like he'd declared his undying love for her. He hadn't done anything to imply any romantic involvement in his feelings. People loved all sorts of things. Cats, dogs, flowers in springtime. So why did her heart just do a handspring in her chest?

● ● ● ●

"You know," his wife slid her arm around his waist, "it's not nice to keep secrets from people."

"I know." Fiona Hart was the one person in the world he'd never kept secrets from. Well, mostly never. "There are times when it's in the best interest of the troops to keep some information on a need to know basis."

"Hmm. I'm not sure I agree on this one. How do you think she'll react when she learns there's more to our monthly trips than a specialty yarn shop?"

"And who's going to tell her?" He loved his wife more than

anything in this world, and trusted her with his life. Smiling down at her, he pulled her closer into the fold of his arm. "If all continues on track, she'll never know. None of them will."

"Marines," she muttered, leaning into him.

"I love you too."

# CHAPTER FOURTEEN

Kids were everywhere. Jake had thought the barbecue was only for the girls on the team, but apparently the invitation included boyfriends, classmates, and family members. The Point was covered with lounge chairs, folding chairs, blankets, and children of all sizes scurrying about chasing balls, dogs, and each other. Jake hadn't had this much fun in years.

"How do you like your steak?" the General asked from a huge barrel smoker.

Jake eyed the grill carefully. He was pretty sure it was the same one the family had used when he was a kid. A huge halved metal barrel painted silver with a grilling screen across the top burned mesquite and charcoal. The thing had made the best burgers in New England. Just looking at the sizzling meat made his mouth water. "Thought we were doing burgers and hot dogs?"

The General waved his arm in the direction of the opposite side of the Point where Floyd manned a carbon copy of the massive grill. "Adults get the good stuff."

He didn't know about that. The burgers he remembered were pretty darn good. "Medium works for me."

"Attaboy." The General smiled. "No sense in ruining a good cut of meat by turning it into boot leather."

"No, sir." Jake resisted the urge to stand at parade rest. Although in his *Grill King* apron the General looked like any other guy at any other family barbecue, but there was still an heir of authority that Jake felt whenever he was with the man. Somehow today running the show with military precision, Jake felt it all the more so. "Anything I can do?"

"Nope. Go enjoy yourself."

That wouldn't be hard. He'd already played horseshoes and tetherball with Heather and concluded that the woman was an ace at whatever she put her mind to. Like yesterday, when it had taken only a few tries to master pulling up on skis, today she'd gone from novice horseshoe tosser to beating him at his own game. He'd made it halfway across the Point when the hairs on the back of his neck prickled. In Lawford the worst that could possibly happen would be if the General overcooked the steaks or Lily forgot to bring dessert. Shaking it off, he changed direction towards the house. Heather and her cousins were inside. Everything was probably fine but still, he didn't like the sensation still pricking at him.

A crowd of hungry teens had formed near Floyd. The call of hotdogs and burgers was an especially powerful siren to growing boys. Shifting direction, he stopped beside Floyd. "I'm heading to the house. Need anything?"

"Everything." Floyd waved his spatula at the grill. "Doesn't anyone ever feed these kids?"

"As a former teenager, it's been my experience that growing boys have a lot in common with dogs."

"Huh?" Floyd grunted.

"As long as you keep offering them food, they'll keep eating."

"Sounds about right." Floyd flipped the last of the burgers and handed Jake the empty dish. "Here you go."

Truth was, he was delighted to have a legitimate excuse to go inside and see Heather. Earlier fun and games hadn't lasted long enough. Tomorrow she would be returning to Boston and then what?

• • • •

"I'd forgotten how much teenagers eat." Lucy pulled bags of hot dog buns from the pantry. "Good thing we have Katie's home phone number."

"I hate to make her open up on a Sunday." Grams had her head in the fridge. "Are we out of mayonnaise?"

Heather held up an empty jar. "Emptied it in this batch of potato salad." She'd hoped to find a few moments to slip away and talk to Jake unfettered by prying eyes, but every time she'd set foot outdoors, something would happen to send her back into the bustling kitchen.

"Floyd needs more of everything."

"Everything?" Lucy snapped around from her position at the

sink.

From the shock in her eyes, Floyd clearly wasn't the only one caught off guard by the football team's appetite.

"I'll call Katie." Fiona Hart crossed the kitchen and grabbing the wall phone, stretched the cord around the doorway.

"I should have known Hart House would still have a land line on the kitchen wall."

Heather wiped her hands on her apron. "How are you holding up?"

"Me?" His voice lowered so only she could hear. "Fine, but I was hoping to get a few minutes with you. Can we take a—"

"Bless that woman." Grams hung the receiver in place and spun about. "She'll have the order packed and ready by the time someone gets to the One Stop."

"I'll go," Heather volunteered. A change of pace would be good. Besides. She faced Jake again. "Want to come for a ride?"

The expansive grin that took over his face and lit his eyes was all the answer she needed.

"Good. Let's go before we get waylay—"

"Ice, please." Practically dragging Floyd with her, Callie came hurrying through the doorway. "Cold water too."

"How bad is it?" Heather took a long step in their direction.

"If I can get it under cold water and ice, it probably won't even blister."

"Ice coming up," Poppy called from near the fridge.

"Let me—"

Lucy waved her off. "You hit the One Stop. If there's anything this old gal can handle it's a little burn. Go."

Heather managed a quick peek and agreed, this was definitely something her family could handle without her.

"There's a crowd of hungry boys out there," Floyd grumbled, yanking his arm away from Lucy. "Just give me some butter and let me get back to my post."

"Butter," Lucy grumbled, the censure clear in her tone.

"I'll man the grill," Jake said to Floyd, then turned to Heather. "Sorry," he mouthed.

Yeah. So was she.

• • • •

Diligently manning his new post, Jake had run out of hamburgers and was doling out the last few hot dogs.

"Any more news on Ralph?" Susie was next in line.

"All good." He was happy to report. "Dr. Preston spoke with him this morning and he's doing better than fine."

"Oh that's good." She held out an empty dish. "This one is for my brother."

If Jake remembered correctly, Susie's older brother was a star on the football team. One of the ones who no doubt was a contributing factor to why only hot dogs were left until Heather returned from the grocery run. "Only one?"

"Yes, sir. The General said only one at a time until Dr. Preston returns."

Smart man, that general, but Jake already knew that. Stabbing at the slender slab of meat, his long laid to rest inner warnings went off again. Taking an extra second to scan the surroundings, he looked for something out of place. Perhaps someone in trouble in the water, or a couple of testosterone-loaded boys in a pissing contest. Nothing. Of course not. He wasn't in the sandbox anymore. What was wrong with him?

The answer to that one was easy. Heather Preston had him totally off balance.

He dropped the hot dog into a bun and set it on the teen's plate. "Here you go."

"Thanks!"

The line of kids eager for a hot dog had dwindled once the announcement had been made that there'd be more burgers shortly. Taking advantage of the lull, he pulled out his phone. There was more than one way to get a few minutes with Heather. Choosing the newly saved number, he waited for her to pick up.

"Thanks again," sounded far away mixed with crumpling sounds and the slamming of a door. "Hello."

"Catching you at a bad time?"

"Oh, hi. Had my hands full and didn't see who was calling." He heard another door slam and an engine come to life. "This is a perfect time. Give me a minute while I put you on speaker."

"Sure." Perfectly content to hear her voice, he'd gladly give her anything she asked for.

• • • •

Heather pulled out of the parking lot and considered what it might be like to hear this voice every day. "I'm back."

"I gather you got everything?"

"Yep. I should be back in ten, fifteen minutes tops. Katie had it all packed and ready for me. She really is a blessing to this town."

"I don't think that woman has an unpleasant bone in her body. I won't be at all surprised to find out one day she's actually an angel."

"Sure bakes like one."

"Yes, she does. So does your cousin."

"Some days, I'm not sure which of them is the better baker, and if you tell Lily I said that I'll swear you're lying!" She held back a giggle. This man brought out a side of her she didn't remember she even had.

"Are there any more hot dogs?" said a female voice Heather was pretty sure belonged to the pretty blonde from last night.

"Hang on," he told Heather. "Absolutely. If you want to wait, Dr. Preston will be back with fixings in about ten minutes or so."

"That's okay. I take it plain."

"All right. Here you go."

"Thanks."

A few more seconds passed before Jake spoke again. "Whoever heard of anyone eating a plain hot dog?"

Heather laughed. "I'm a dash of mustard and smidge of relish girl myself."

"Smidge, huh?" Jake laughed and the sound ricocheted through her like a high alcohol tonic. "Susie!" he suddenly shouted without moving the phone away from him.

Heather didn't like the sound of it.

"Are you…crap."

# CHAPTER FIFTEEN

"**D**amn it."

Walking along the edge of the foot-wide retaining wall keeping the Point high above the creek and lake, Susie suddenly dropped the hot dog and her hands flew to her neck. It was the wide-eyed look of terror so stark he could see it clear from across the Point that spiked his blood pressure seconds before she wilted like a flower and plummeted over the side.

For a short moment Jake would have sworn his heart stopped. Apparently the only one who'd seen her distress, he tossed the phone and lunged in her direction. There was no way in hell he could reach her in time to stop the splash of icy water jetting high into the air.

The desperate pitch in Jake's voice and the splash seconds later had heads turning. Poppy standing with a handful of parents near the edge of the Point tore off toward the house and shouted. "I'll get a towel."

Jake prayed a towel was the only thing the sweet kid would need. Except coming to a screeching halt at the same ledge the young girl had been balancing on only seconds before, his heart took another dive. Susie was floating face down in the icy water.

● ● ● ●

"Jake!" Heather shouted into the phone.

"Hello?" a ragged breath followed the single word.

"What's going on?" Heather demanded in the military tone she'd inherited from her grandfather.

"Susie fell in the lake." The breathless voice belonged to Lily. "Jake's gone in after her."

"After her? The water is freezing. Why doesn't she just climb...wait...what do you mean fell?"

"I mean she was eating a hotdog, walking along the edge toe to toe. You know the way a drunk walks toe to toe in a sobriety line."

Heather nodded even though no one could see.

"One minute she was munching along and the next she was gone and Jake was sprinting in her direction."

*Oh no. Lord no.* For the second time in so many days a multitude of worse case scenarios flew through Heather's mind. "Is she okay?"

"I don't know. They haven't come back up yet," she panted. "I'm almost there."

*Blast.* Helping the young girl out of the water and up the wall is one thing. Carrying out an injured one is another. For all she knew both of them were hurt. Now her heart rate was galloping like a thoroughbred at the finish line. "Tell me exactly what's going on."

"I can't see," Lily's voice came out low and sketchy, "Wait. Here he comes. Oh God, Heather she's out cold. And bleeding."

"Bleeding where?"

"Anyone here with medical background?" Jake shouted loud enough for Heather to hear him.

"Get me next to him and put me on speakerphone." Heather could feel the nervous energy through the phone line.

"Hang on, he's got his arms around her doing the Heimlich." Lily huffed out of breath from running.

"The Heimlich? What is going on?" Lily didn't respond. *Damn it.* "Can anyone hear me?"

"I can," he answered. "I think she was choking and passed out before she fell, but I can't get anything to pop out and she's not coming to."

"Is she breathing at all?"

"She has a small gash on her forehead." Jake answered quickly. "But her color is washed away and her lips are starting to turn blue. Hang on."

"He's putting his hand on her chest and his cheek to her face," Lily spoke up.

"I don't think she's breathing," Jake said in a rush. "But I can feel her heart beat. Barely."

"If she passed out from lack of oxygen she must have an obstruction."

"I don't know," Jake said. "I'm sticking my finger in as far as I

128 CHRIS KENISTON

can, I don't feel anything."

*Blast.* Heather sucked in a deep breath, gripping the phone more tightly. "There's no other choice. She needs air. You only have a couple of minutes. You'll have to do a tracheotomy."

"Cut her?" This time true panic laced Jake's words.

Heather nodded. "Yes! She needs air. I'll talk you through it." She'd never phoned in surgery before. Panic licked at her own nerves.

"Nine one one has been called. Ambulance is on the way," Jake said in a hurry

"Doesn't matter. There's no time. You have to do this or we'll lose her."

"Okay. Lord help me, but okay."

"We need a sharp knife."

"I've got knives in the kitchen," Lucy's voice carried in the distance.

"I'll get the first aid kit," her grandmother shouted.

"No need, Fiona. Here you go," the General said, his voice even, sturdy. Bless him, the voice of calm, he must have already gone for the first aid kit to give Jake.

"Wait," Jake's voice sounded stronger. "I have a Leatherman tool. It has a pocket knife."

"You need something for a small tube."

Another second of silence hung before Jake muttered "straw" followed by a loud, "Give me that cup."

She didn't know who he was pointing to but she hoped whoever it was didn't have an ordinary straw that wouldn't hold up to the pressure.

"I've got one of those sturdy hard plastic straws from a large water bottle."

"Good. You have to work fast. There should be some alcohol in the first aid kit to sterilize her neck."

"Got it," he said.

"Look for a notch at the base of her throat, about where her chest starts. In the middle."

"Found it."

"Good. Now make a two inch vertical incision through the skin."

"I need a ruler!" he shouted.

"We don't have time," she hollered back. "Eyeball it!"

She could almost swear she could hear him and every other person on the Point swallow hard. "There's going to be a bit of blood but that's okay. You have to open the skin with your fingers and keep cutting until you see a couple of horizontal rings of tissue."

"I think I found it."

"Make an incision between the rings of tissue and stick the straw in the hole you make. The tissue is fibrous. It won't be easy to cut. Ignore the blood and just get the straw in there."

"Oh heaven," Lily mumbled, "he's doing it."

"The skin seemed to seal itself around the tube," Jake almost whispered. She could hear the awe in his voice.

A hint of pride pulled at one side of her lips. "That's what's supposed to happen. Is she breathing?"

"Yes," relief sounded in his voice.

"Good. Pack cotton from the kit around the wound." Now she smiled in earnest. "You did it."

Sirens sounded in the distance.

"Sounds like the ambulance is almost there. I'll drop the supplies off and then go check on her."

"If you don't mind," he blew out a heavy breath, "I think from now on I'll leave the surgery to you."

"We'll take it from here," a voice she didn't recognize, most likely the EMTs, instructed.

She could hear the commotion of instructions and movement as the EMTs checked the girl's vitals and boogied to get her to the hospital.

Not till the sirens again sounded and began to fade into the distance did Jake speak. The muffled sounds of people in the background disappeared, he was no longer on speakerphone. "I'm saying it again. You're amazing."

"Not this time. You did all the work."

"And you do it every day." His sudden chuckle surprised her.

"What?

"I was just thinking. Sometimes you just have to eyeball it."

She laughed with him. "Guess you were right." *About a whole lot of things.*

# CHAPTER SIXTEEN

"You did good, son." General Harold Hart swirled the glass of bourbon in his hand. "I've had to do a lot of difficult things under miserable conditions. I've lost a lot of good men. Boys actually. Thought that was behind me. I'm glad you were here."

"Someone would have stepped up. I just happened to be closest." Jake took a slow sip of the smooth caramel colored drink. Once the party had come to an end after Susie fell into the lake and things had been cleaned up and put away, just about the time the adrenaline rush came crashing down, the General handed him a drink and insisted Jake join him on the porch. Swaying in the big old green rockers, Jake and his nerves agreed the General's idea had merit.

The General swirled his glass again and shook his head. "The majority of guests were under the legal voting age. The only person with that kind of medical training was gone. You were it, son. You came through. Own it."

"Yes, sir."

A plate of pie and ice cream in each hand, Mrs. Hart joined them on the porch. "Nothing like Lily's homemade pie and ice cream from the Creamery to get the endorphins going after a harried day."

Wearing one of her long flowing dresses, Fiona Hart grinned at him. Her accurately scientific explanation of comfort food surprised him. "Thank you."

Callie, Lily and Poppy, followed their grandmother. Within minutes almost the entire family in residence silently rocked, side by side, eating their ice cream.

"Yes, I'll tell her. Uh huh." Violet stepped over the threshold, her phone at her ear, and scanned the area for an empty seat. "I love you too."

"Who is it?" Lily asked.

"Rose. She accidentally butt dialed me."

"Not having any pie?" her grandmother asked.

"No. I need the sugar rush like I need a hole in my head." Violet collapsed on a nearby chair. "I don't ever remember having a day like today, and I hope there's never another one like it."

Bouncing headlights lit up the lake in the distance.

"Oh, I think she's home." Fiona Hart pushed to her feet and Jake realized for the first time all week she hadn't been knitting.

The porch went immediately quiet again. Only the sounds of crickets could be heard over the slamming of a car door. Jake watched the silhouette coming up the walkway. His heart lifted at the first clear sight of Heather. Neither bourbon nor a sugar coma could affect him the way a mere glimpse of her did. Never had he felt so strongly about any woman before, and he was sure that no matter how long he lived, no one could ever compare to Heather Preston.

His gaze tracked her every move. Up the steps. Stretching her arm to open the door. The moment her gaze met his, her lips curled upward in a smile that mirrored the one that had just taken over his face. Damn he loved that smile. Not just the smile. He loved her. Dr. Heather Preston. And wasn't this one helluva time to fall in love.

"How is she?" he asked.

Her eyes remained leveled with his. "She's awake and alert. And moving her toes."

"Moving her toes?" Violet asked.

Heather nodded. "I didn't say anything over the phone. I wasn't terribly concerned about water in her lungs due to the obstruction, but the creek isn't that deep near the wall. I didn't know exactly where she went over and was a little concerned with potential spinal injuries."

His heart gave a stutter. "I moved her like a rag doll."

"You had no choice. There was no time. Spinal injury was secondary to not dying. All of which is a moot point as she's fine. "

"I love good news." Fiona pushed out of her seat. "I'll get you some pie and ice cream."

"Sounds heavenly."

He wasn't sure when he'd stood, and he had no idea when the others had abandoned their chairs to follow Fiona. All he knew was there was no looking away from Heather. Nothing seemed to matter more this minute than holding her in his arms and keeping her safe and close. Preferably forever.

"You may have missed your calling in life." Heather came to a stop in front of him. "You saved her life."

"*You* saved her life." He ran his hands along the sides of her arms. "I would have been useless without you." His own words echoed in his head. Deep in his heart he knew as sure as he knew his own name that the rest of his life wouldn't be worth the paper his birth certificate was printed on without her in it.

• • • •

All Heather had wanted from the moment the ER doctor confirmed Susie was stable and out of danger was to get home and find Jake. *Home. Jake.* Funny how the two words fit together so well. Not Boston, not the hospital, not surgery. Home and Jake. She was sure if she said them out loud they would easily roll off her tongue. And wasn't that just her luck.

She wasn't sure how long she'd stood merely steps away. She wasn't sure when her family had cleared the porch leaving only the two of them. And she couldn't remember when she'd been so afraid to move. Afraid everything she felt inside would come pouring out. Afraid that a single touch would tell him every scrambled emotion coursing through her veins. Not even for her first surgery had she been so afraid that even one wrong word or move could screw up the rest of her life.

Crickets continued to chirp. An owl gave a low hoot off in the distance. And the clacking of paws on wooden floors grew closer. People were coming. Heather sucked in a deep breath, prepared to retreat, to organize her thoughts and determine how she could feel so very much for one person in such a short amount of time.

The clacking quickened and two golden blurs appeared in her peripheral vision. Where Lady and Sarge went, the General was soon to follow. About to step back, she froze when the warmth of the dog's fur brushed against the back of her legs. As soon as she felt the fluff of a swishing tail slide away from one leg, a cold nose bumped against the other.

"Whoa." Surprise ringing in his voice, Jake took a single step forward wobbling for balance.

At the same moment, the full weight of a seventy-pound golden retriever suddenly rammed against the back of her knees sending Heather flying the remainder of the short distance between them, slamming her against a rock solid chest. Strong hands circled around her arms, steadying her.

"Hi, there," the low timbre of his voice sent shock waves rippling through her system. "Fancy meeting you here."

"Lady, Sarge, heel," the General's voice boomed from inside the house and two sets of paws clacked a rapid beat against the solid surface floors and into the distance.

"Sounds like they went AWOL," he chuckled.

"More like rogue."

His face lit up. "I'm glad. Well, not that they disobeyed orders, but that they pushed me to take a step."

Heather glanced down from left to right and then over to the doorway. "That was a bit odd of them."

"They seem to like getting under our feet." His hands settled easily on her hips.

Something about what he'd just said had her wanting to think, to process, to say something, but the fog seeping into her brain from his nearness wouldn't have let her recite the alphabet, never mind form any intelligent conversation.

"I was just thinking."

She was glad someone could think.

"I have a college roommate who lives in Winchester. Haven't seen him for a few years."

"Oh." Her heart was picking up speed.

He nodded. "If I made my way down one weekend to visit do you think you might be able to free up a few hours for dinner?"

This time her head bobbed. "Everyone has to eat."

"Maybe dancing?" His lips curved in a smile.

The memory of the other night had her heaving a small sigh. "I'd like that."

"Next weekend?" he asked.

"I'd like that too."

His mouth met hers, pressing lightly at first, and then creating a dance all their own. She definitely liked that. Actually, she loved it. Loved him. The thought should have scared the bejeezus out of her, but it didn't. All she wanted was to stand in this spot for the next twenty or thirty years kissing this man.

When his lips pulled away from hers, she tightened her hold around his waist and bit back the words, *don't stop*.

He let his forehead slowly come to rest on hers and blew out a small breath. She had the feeling they were both doing their best to steady rapid heart rates. Hanging onto her, his head lifted back and his eyes leveled with hers. "This may be a mistake, but I'm going to say it anyhow."

Praying he didn't say he'd changed his mind about coming to visit, she was already running options for coming to see him instead, almost surprising herself at the thought of going to talk with the local hospital about taking on a cardiac surgeon. She waited for sanity to strike that thought down, but instead found the idea taking root.

Placing his finger under her chin, he lifted her face to meet his. The sharpness in his eyes left her breathless. "I love you."

Her heart skipped a wild beat. Words like that should drive a woman on her career track running away as fast as she could. Instead they made her smile. "That could be a good thing."

He cocked one brow. "Could?"

"Yeah," she nodded. "Because I'm pretty sure I love you too."

An echoed thumping sounded beside them. Heather glanced down at her feet. Lady sat to one side of them, Sarge on the other, tails wagging a mile a minute against the hard porch floor. If Heather didn't know better she'd swear the two animals were smiling at them.

Jake looked from the dogs to her, his forehead scrunched in a slight frown. "Do you think they know something we don't?"

Wrapping her hand around his neck, she pulled him in for a quick touch of the lips, then smiled up at him. "Not anymore."

# CHAPTER SEVENTEEN

"There's a reason the dining room was designed as the biggest room in the house. Lots of offspring." Left hand on her hip, Lucy counted the chairs with her free hand. "Good thing, too, or there wouldn't be enough for this brood."

"How many times are you going to do that?" Grams shook her head, placing the bacon-wrapped asparagus tips on the buffet. "Two tables seating for eighteen. We've got this covered."

A tray in each hand, Lily set the deviled eggs and Swedish meatballs beside the other appetizers and chuckled at the two women. She didn't know of many families who kept a spare drop leaf dining table just for holiday dinners. "It is rather fun having all of us together, no excuses."

"Well, we have been doing this every year since you girls were twinkles in your parent's eyes." Grams smiled at her granddaughter.

"Yes." Lucy spun around to face Lily. "But this year there is an extra seat at the table."

"They do seem rather happy, don't they?" Lily didn't have to be clairvoyant to know why Lucy was especially excited this year. What she didn't understand was how Heather had pulled it off. Ever since falling for Jake Harper she had managed to come to the lake every other weekend. On opposite weekends, Jake had gone to Boston. With each visit to the lake, the two looked more in sync than the time before. Any minute now Lily expected them to finish each other's sentences. Or even still, read each other's minds. Though, frankly, she wasn't totally sure they weren't already doing that.

"Where shall I put these?" Iris held out a tray of kolackys and another of spitzbuben.

"Those are for dessert." Lily sighed. She'd better put the crème puffs and coconut custard pie away before one of her family brought those out too.

"Oh no. These are meant to be snacked on all day long." Iris maneuvered the trays away from Lily. "Thanksgiving is all about leaving the diets and the calorie counting behind. Technically it's the one day of the year where nothing counts."

"Do you want the cheese platters in here or in the parlor?" Cindy balanced her grandmother's garlic cheese ball and her grandfather's favorite jalapeno jam on cream cheese spread.

"Is everyone in the States of New York and Massachusetts joining us for dinner?" Dragging her roller bag behind her, Zinnia parked it against the wall and stuffing her gloves in her pockets, hurried into her grandmother's arms. "Boy, are you a sight for sore eyes."

"Stop the presses," Cindy called. "The prodigal cousin has returned."

"Ha ha." Zinnia let go of her grandmother and twisted around to hug her cousin.

"Nice to have you back."

"Ditto," Zinnia murmured.

Tails wagging, Sarge and Lady came running, nails clacking on the hardwood floors.

"Everyone is happy to see you." The General followed the pups and swallowed his granddaughter in an old-fashioned bear hug.

Multiple footsteps fell heavily on the front porch. Immediately, Lucy beamed and elbowed Grams, whispering like a giddy teen, "They're here."

Lily would have rolled her eyes except she was just as excited to see her cousin and her 'beau' as Lucy called him. She liked that at least someone in the family had finally found a match to equal what they'd grown up with.

Heather came through the door, stomping snowy boots on the winter welcome mat. One hand linked with Jake's, she grinned at the cluster of family hovering in the massive foyer. "Now this is what I call a welcoming committee." Slowly, her fingers slipped away from Jake's as he helped her shrug out of her coat.

On her way to the kitchen, Lily caught Jake's eye and reading the silent question, nodded. His responding grin was so bright she was rather surprised no one else in the room noticed.

Everything about today just made Lily want to smile. The special cupcakes were safely tucked away so none of the other family members would pilfer them. As much as she loved baking, this particular project had filled her day with joy, and maybe a pinch of envy, but mostly joy and happiness for her oldest cousin.

"That man seems too good to be true." Violet slid onto a stool at the island. "How did none of us notice him before?"

"Because he wasn't meant for any of us."

Grinning, Violet reached for a box of crackers. "True."

"If you're going to loiter in here," Lucy hurried into the kitchen and pointed toward the back wall, "grab an apron and help with the food."

"Yes, ma'am." Violet sprang to her feet. "But for the sake of the ER, you'd better only be needing help with salad."

Lily couldn't help but laugh. As much as she'd love to accuse her cousin of exaggerating, sadly, the kitchen was definitely not Violet's friend.

"On second thought," Lucy wiped her hands on her side, "this can wait. Let's join everyone in the parlor."

"Good idea." Violet set the apron she'd grabbed back on the hook.

Within the hour all the cousins and their parents were scattered around the first floor eating and laughing and sharing favorite memories.

"Well," the General stood from his favorite chair, "I, for one, am ready for some turkey."

Cindy pushed to her feet. "And just a heads up, I helped with the gravy."

Half the room moaned, the other half laughed, and following the General to the dining room, Lily and Cindy's mom patted her daughter on the back. "Don't worry, sweetie, if having a doctor in the family doesn't help, I know a good funeral director."

Winding her arm around her mom's waist, Cindy smiled. "I love you too."

Coming up behind them, Heather patted her cousin on the back as well. "No worries, I have connections at the local hospital. We can pump stomachs in a heartbeat."

"Ha ha ha." Cindy took it all with the good humor intended.

Standing behind Heather, Jake caught Lily's attention and nodded.

Lily flashed him a thumbs up and slipped away from the crowd to the cupboard where she'd hid the requested confection.

With eighteen people shuffling around the table either finding seats or carrying in food from the kitchen, no one noticed Lily entering the room with the dish of elaborate cupcakes. While everybody settled down in their seats, Lily placed a red velvet cupcake with cream cheese icing and a single candle sticking up.

It took a few minutes of additional chatting for most folks to even realize what she'd done.

Heather finally stopped gazing into Jake's eyes long enough to notice the cupcake. "What's this? It's not my birthday?"

"They say," Jake cleared his throat, "that to enjoy life to the fullest, we should have dessert first."

Blinking, Heather's gaze scanned the room and noticed she was the only one with a cupcake. Looking down, her eyes suddenly widened giving away when she spotted the brilliant cut diamond ring hanging off the candle.

Her startled gasp, coupled with Jake's chair scraping the floor as he pushed away from the table to get down on one knee, silenced the few family members still catching up.

Tears filled Heather's eyes. Even knowing what was coming, Lily had to blink back her own tears of happiness for her cousin.

"I know this isn't as romantic as a sunrise proposal on the point, but if you say yes, I promise to love you with all my heart and to spend every day giving my all to make you happy. Will you marry me?"

To say Heather flew out of the chair would be the understatement of the century. The seat kicked back, and throwing her arms around Jake's neck, the two toppled over onto the floor.

"I do believe that is a yes." The General smiled.

Heather leaned back, and grinning from ear to ear, called over her shoulder, "That is a resounding yes."

One not so quick kiss later, Jake and Heather came to their feet.

Already seated beside Heather, Lily was the first to huddle around her cousin with a congratulatory hug. Squeals of oh my gosh, congratulations, and I want to see the ring, tumbled over each other until Jake reached around her and removing the ring from the candle, held it up to her. "May I?"

Heather bobbed her head, grinning like a fool.

Taking a second to wipe some of the icing from the diamond, Jake slid it onto the third finger of her left hand. "I'm sorry it's a little messy. Still want to marry me?"

"Absolutely." Her grin growing impossibly wider, she nodded at her new fiancé. "Life doesn't get any better than this."

Sitting down again, while the rest of the family continued to drench Heather with more squeals and hugs, and shook Jake's hand with congratulations and the occasional warning, Lily wistfully took in the scene. Who knew on that night not so long ago when Heather collided with Jake at the bottom of the stairs, that her world would never be the same.

Too bad the only thing Lily ever collided with was usually low to the ground and unlikely to be breathing. And wasn't that a shame.

# From Lily's Recipe Box

## CREAM CHEESE KOLACKY

What you'll need:

6-ounce cake of cream cheese
½ lb butter (2 sticks)
2 cups flour
Strawberry/Blueberry or other preserves

Instructions:

Cream butter and cream cheese.
Gradually stir in flour.
Chill thoroughly 1-2 hours.
Roll very thin.
Cut out with small glass or cutter.
Place on ungreased cookie sheet.
Press center with finger.
Add preserves (¼ teaspoon or whatever amount of preserves that will fit into the pressed center).
Bake at 350 degrees for 10 minutes or until slightly browned.
Let cool and sprinkle with powdered sugar.


Lily's note: *These should not be too large as they are very rich.*

# Excerpt from LILY

*"It will never work."*
*"Of course, it will."*
*"As much as I'd like to think you're right, I don't know."*
*"Well, I do. Sit back and see for yourself."*

Flames thrashed at the charred walls. Time was running out. Pushing through the thick black smoke, Cole McIntyre made his way down the second floor hall of the small high school, checking and clearing each and every classroom along the way. According to the teachers huddled outside, there was one teacher and possibly two or three students trapped behind the fire line. Even in the few minutes it had taken them to weave through the afternoon traffic, the small fire had grown to engulf half the building.

Every thirty seconds this monster was doubling in size. Despite the protective gear, Cole could feel the heat beating at his back. What a mess. The snap of crumbling wood sounded overhead. A flaming beam came crashing down, sending him jagging left—fast.

"Cole!" His partner's voice sounded in his ear.

Flashing a thumbs up, Cole pressed forward. Neither able to see more than a few feet in front of them, he'd counted doors and had to be approaching the chemistry lab at the end of the hall. A student who had escaped from the lab reported the flash fire had climbed instantly to the ceiling and rapidly traveled toward the back wall, trapping the teacher and whoever had been sitting nearby. Afraid to cross through the flames, the teacher herded the children to temporary safety in a storage room. He hoped to God the door was made of steel.

In an attempt to contain the fire, several teachers had pulled the doors closed behind them on their way out of the building. The chem lab had been no exception. Kicking the door down and staying low, he followed the wall around for reference. The outside team had been watering down this area but the lab was still a hot spot. Heart rate pounding, he came to the storage room and shoved the door open.

In the opposite corner, the teacher and one student lay close to the ground. Before he could reach them, the two crawled, one hand holding their faces, in his direction. They were alive. Now came the fun part—getting them the hell out of the building.

• • • •

"I. Am. Not. Frustrated." Lily Nelson blew a wisp of hair away from her face and slammed her fist into the gooey mound in front of her.

"Call it what you want." Hands on her hips, Lucy, the family's longtime housekeeper, cook, and avid Hello Dolly fan, stared at her with cool indifference. "I've watched you bake bread before and you don't usually pound at the dough with quite so much murderous intent."

Lily flipped and folded the dough, making a conscious effort to not hammer at it as if it were Danny Fluegel's face.

"I don't suppose you want to tell me why you're baking bread here at this hour?"

"This kitchen is bigger than Mom's." The timer sounded and wiping her hands on her apron, Lily crossed the room, ignoring the woman standing guard like a drill sergeant at boot camp, and peeked into the oven. Perfection. Using her apron for mitts, she maneuvered the hot tray onto the cooling rack and spun back to the raw dough.

So what if she baked when she had too much on her mind? So what if Danny Fluegel went out last night with featherbrained—and stacked—Kathleen Barker? It's not like they were in a committed relationship. Heck, after only three dates in three weeks she wasn't even sure it counted as a relationship. And even if he was perfect-picture- handsome, after two rather wilted kisses, she hadn't even been sure she wanted a fourth date.

What she wanted was her own bakery. A place to create all the delectable flavors swirling in her head for the rest of the world to taste and enjoy. Or at least all of Lawford mountain not staying at the Hilltop Inn. And Margaret O'Malley's Boutique on Main Street would be the perfect spot. Just not this year. She punched the dough again.

"Oh, my." Either not noticing or choosing to overlook the last act of violence on the innocent pile of raw dough, Lucy inched closer to the warm French breakfast fare, sniffed the air as though she were a blood hound on the hunt, and moaned softly. "I have no idea what has sent you into baker-on-steroids mode, but I do love your croissants. Is that extra butter I smell?"

Lily might have gotten a little heavy handed with the butter. But to her, butter was the basis of all great comfort foods. And tonight she felt like comfort.

Visiting from Boston, her cousin Violet stopped short in the doorway. "Do I smell croissants?"

"With extra butter." Lucy snuck a pinch of the steaming warm flaky temptation.

Lily blew out a sigh and returned her fingers to the dough.

"You going to bake that or beat five pounds out of it?" Violet pinched a morsel of croissant for herself. A yoga instructor, her cousin had the calm Zen life down pat. "Cause if you need to get rid of some of that frustration, I could show you—"

"I am not frustrated." Miffed. Disappointed, maybe. But not frustrated. Not really. Maybe. All right. Who was she kidding? Self-absorbed men like Danny were made for the Barbie look-alikes in this world. She should have known better than to let Lucy set her up, but with Heather and Jake looking so insanely happy, and her not having been on a single date in two years, she might have been a bit too willing to overlook Lucy's track record. Being dumped—sort of—by him wouldn't have bothered her at all if she didn't see her biggest chance at her own bakery slipping away.

"Then tell me why you look like your soufflé fell?" Barefoot, dressed in comfy yoga pants and an oversized t-shirt, her cousin leaned against the counter, silently waiting for Lily to explain her late night baking marathon.

Heaving a sigh, she dropped the dough in a bowl, covered it with a towel, and turned to her audience of two. "Danny Fluegel is seeing Kathleen Barker."

"The man has no taste." Lucy stuffed another piece of croissant in her mouth as if she hadn't been the one to set Lily and Danny up in the first place.

Violet frowned. "I thought he was a bad kisser?'

"He is."

"Then I don't understand." The frown remained intact.

"It's just…" What? Danny. No. That was a handy excuse. If only the timing wasn't all wrong.

Shaking her head and smiling, Lucy came up to Lily and patted her hand before stepping away again. "If it makes you feel any better, we've got a few bookings coming up with new guests. Including a handsome fireman."

"Lucy," Lily practically groaned

"What?" Lucy's not so innocent eyes opened wide. "You have anything against good looking firemen?"

"Of course not. But I don't want you saying—or doing—anything that I'm going to regret." Again. Lucy may think herself the matchmaker extraordinaire but there was no denying how terrible she was at it. Not only, like Danny, did her choices not pan out, her methods were questionable. Last summer the woman had actually tripped Amy Crowder at the Fourth of July barbecue so Lucy could insist the new—six foot two, blue eyed, good looking—EMT take a look at Amy's not sprained ankle. She didn't need Lucy arranging yet another date for her with a self-absorbed, too-handsome for his own good, member of the male species. Someone could get hurt.

"Me?" Lucy had the audacity to flatten her palm against her chest and look surprised at being called out on her matchmaking shenanigans. "I haven't done a thing. A fire department representative will stay with us for a week to decide if Hart Land would be a good spot for the annual firefighter's retreat. Between the lake views, my cooking, and your baking, there isn't a snowball's chance under the sun the retreat won't be held here."

On the surface that seemed like a legitimate reason for having a firefighter in one of the rental cabins. After all, ever since his class reunion several months ago, her grandfather, retired Marine Corps General Harold Hart, had been practically living on the computer strategizing new marketing efforts the same way she suspected he would have planned the invasion of an enemy country. Both of which she had no doubt he would be successful at. On the other hand, this was Lucy.

Pulling apart another croissant, the housekeeper paused mid-tear and grinned. "Can you imagine all those good looking firemen scattered across Hart Land for days?"

"Luuucy," Lily enunciated carefully.

The older woman swiped another croissant and turned away, mumbling, "Sometimes I think you girls are the baby boomers and your Grams and I are the younger generation."

"Well, you're both certainly young at heart, I'll give you that." And that was all Lily was going to say. Otherwise Lucy was capable of setting a cabin on fire so the big strong firemen could rescue her damsel in distressed self.

Waiting a beat for Lucy to be out of earshot, Violet cleared her throat. "Okay, it's just the two of us. What's really eating at you and don't tell me it's Danny because I'm not buying."

"Okay." Lily sank onto a stool and considered if half past eleven was too late to test a new recipe for butterscotch cookies she'd been thinking about. Oh just spit it out. "Margaret O'Malley is retiring."

"Heaven knows she's probably older than dirt." Having grown up in Boston, Violet and her two sisters had spent every summer at the lake and knew all the locals as well as any resident of Lawford.

"She told Mom that without Herbie, running the shop just wouldn't be the same. She's going to close the boutique." Lily reached for a croissant.

"That's wonderful." Violet leaped forward and stopped short at Lily's expression. "Isn't it? I mean, you've been dreaming of your own bakery on Main Street for years."

Dreaming was the key word. Since returning from studying in France she'd scrimped and saved, moved in with her mom, and to save even more money, spent most of her free evenings on her grandparent's porch playing cards with the retired generation and miscellaneous cabin guests. Getting out the last few weeks—even with Danny Fluegel—had been a nice change.

"I give," Violet said. "Why isn't this good news? The shops on Main Street never turn over. We all thought it would be years before you got your chance."

Years. It seemed that might be how long it could take to find that one signature item to set her apart from the rest of the bakeries in the state. Seeking the elusive standout cupcake, cookie, cake, or bread recipe, this kitchen had been through more experiments than a high-tech chemistry lab searching for a cancer cure. With the cost of remodeling and no single standout marketable hook, she didn't have enough savings to keep her afloat past the first year. If that. "It's just not the best timing."

"Timing?"

"I'm not ready."

"Ready?" Violet's eyes circled round with surprise. "You do remember you're a graduate of the best cooking school in Paris? You've been ready for this since you were eight years and old and got your first Easy Bake Oven."

That made her smile. "Ten and my second Easy Bake Oven. I wore out the first one."

"See. You can do this. If you want to."

Yeah. She wanted to. Boy, did she want to.

• • • •

"Man, that could have been so much worse." Cole's partner Payton guzzled a bottle of cool water.

Cole dropped hard onto the wooden chair in the kitchen. "What's the point of the US Chemical Safety Board—a federal agency—warning against using methanol in laboratory and school demonstrations if the teachers aren't going to pay any attention?"

Rolling the cool bottle across his forehead, Payton shrugged. "Don't ask me, ask the school board."

"At least she had the good sense to block the bottom of the door with towels."

"Didn't hurt any that they were breathing through…what was it?"

"A cotton slip." Cole had to give the woman credit for staying calm in a situation that would have sent most people into a deadly panic. "She'd taken hers off and torn it in pieces for them to breathe through."

Payton narrowed his eyes. "I thought only grandmothers wore those things."

"Apparently not."

"Whatever." Payton jumped to his feet and crossed to the stove. "My stomach is about to kiss my backbone. How much longer?"

Derrick, the firefighter in charge of dinner tonight, didn't bother answering. He just shot Payton an annoyed glare, much like a big brother would to his nuisance younger sibling.

Swiping a slice of bread from the basket on the counter, Payton turned back to his partner. "So how did you get this sweet assignment?"

"What assignment?" Gabe, the charmer of the firehouse, came to a stop by the kitchen table.

Payton waived his thumb at Cole. "This one is spending an all expenses paid week's stay on the Hart property by the lake."

Gabe whistled. "I'm with Bruiser here. How'd you finagle that?"

"I didn't finagle anything. Captain asked if I'd volunteer a day off to inspect all the smoke alarms on the property. Next thing I know, the old guy—"

"You mean the General?" Derrick asked.

Cole nodded. "That would be the one. Followed me around closer than my shadow. Any minute I thought the guy was going to tell me how to do my job."

"You mean he didn't?" Derrick looked surprised.

"Nope. He frowned, harrumphed a few times, might have cracked a hint of a smile a time or two, but refrained from critiquing my performance." Before any of the guys could come back with a wise crack, he responded, "And no comments from the peanut gallery. My performance is just fine."

"All I know," Derrick pulled out the chair beside him, "is that when I did that inspection two years ago the guy was worse than white on rice. Questioned if I needed a different screwdriver—a screwdriver—then he questioned the accuracy of the meters. Anyone would have thought testing smoke alarms required a PhD in rocket science."

Cole chuckled. "Maybe you have a dishonest face?"

Turning away from Derrick, Payton swallowed a grin. Cole would have expected him to be the first to jump on a line like that.

"Hardy har har," Derrick flashed a toothy smile. "I haven't heard of anyone ever getting invited back, never mind invited to stay for a week."

"It's not like he wants to play poker with me. Hart House wants the retreat business."

"And what," Gabe frowned, "would you have to do with that?"

Cole shrugged. "Honestly, I don't know. I was just as shocked as you guys are when the captain called me into his office to inform me of the stay."

"Isn't it against department policy to accept gifts?" Derrick ran a hand across the back of his neck. "I mean, a week's stay at a popular lakeside vacation spot, even between peak seasons, is one hell of a gift."

Payton nodded. "He's got a point."

"Again," Cole repeated, "I have no idea. For all I know there isn't a fire chief in the state willing to go against the General. Whatever the reason, starting tomorrow, like it or not, I'll be taking my vacation in Hart Land."

"Do you get to bring a guest?" An impish grin teased at one side of Payton's mouth. "A week on the water with a hot date could have its advantages."

"Dude, the guy is going on the invite of a retired United States Marine Corps general." Derrick waved a wooden spoon in Cole's direction. "I don't think the General's looking for the guy to turn the cabin into party city."

The sly grin slipped from Payton's face.

Like Cole had said before, he was about to spend a long week of restful solitude on the lake, whether he liked it or not.

**Available at your favorite bookseller.**

# MEET CHRIS

*USA TODAY* Bestselling Author of more than a dozen contemporary novels, including the award-winning *Champagne Sisterhood*, Chris Keniston lives in suburban Dallas with her husband, two human children, and two canine children. Though she loves her puppies equally, she admits being especially attached to her German Shepherd rescue. After all, even dogs deserve a happily ever after.

**More on Chris and her books can be found at**
www.chriskeniston.com

Follow Chris on Facebook at ChrisKenistonAuthor
or on Twitter @ckenistonauthor

**Questions? Comments?**
I would love to hear from you.
You can reach me at chris@chriskeniston.com